Praise for be

Sarah

'Sarah Morgan puts the magic in Christmas'
—*Now* magazine

'Full of romance and sparkle'
—*Lovereading*

'I've found an author I adore—must hunt down
everything she's published.'
—*Smart Bitches, Trashy Books*

'Morgan is a magician with words.'
—*RT Book Reviews*

'Dear Ms Morgan, I'm always on the lookout for
a new book by you…'
—*Dear Author blog*

Sarah Morgan is the bestselling author of *Sleigh Bells in the Snow*. As a child Sarah dreamed of being a writer and, although she took a few interesting detours on the way, she is now living that dream. With her writing career she has successfully combined business with pleasure and she firmly believes that reading romance is one of the most satisfying and fat-free escapist pleasures available. Her stories are unashamedly optimistic and she is always pleased when she receives letters from readers saying that her books have helped them through hard times.

Sarah lives near London with her husband and two children, who innocently provide an endless supply of authentic dialogue. When she isn't writing or reading, Sarah enjoys music, movies and any activity that takes her outdoors.

Readers can find out more about Sarah and her books from her website: www.sarahmorgan.com. She can also be found on Facebook and Twitter.

THE Notting Hill *Diaries*

Ripped & Burned

Sarah Morgan

This edition published in Great Britain 2014
by Mills & Boon, an imprint of Harlequin (UK) Limited,
Eton House, 18-24 Paradise Road, Richmond, Surrey, TW9 1SR

THE NOTTING HILL DIARIES © 2014 by Harlequin Books S.A.

Ripped © 2013 Sarah Morgan
Burned © 2014 Sarah Morgan

COSMOPOLITAN and COSMO are registered trademarks of Hearst Communications, Inc.

ISBN: 978-0-263-24650-6

097-0614

Harlequin (UK) Limited's policy is to use papers that are natural, renewable and recyclable products and made from wood grown in sustainable forests. The logging and manufacturing processes conform to the legal environmental regulations of the country of origin.

Printed and bound by
CPI Group (UK) Ltd, Croydon, CR0 4YY

To Katie, with love.
Have fun and be fearless. Xxxx

Ripped

Dear Reader,

I love writing about strong, independent women and I've always been a lover of *Cosmopolitan*, so when I was asked to write a 'Cosmo Red-Hot Read from Mills & Boon®' story I knew I was going to enjoy myself.

The heroine of *Ripped*, Hayley, is a real Cosmo girl. She's fun, fearless, independent and busy living life to the fullest. She shares an apartment with her sister Rosie, has a job she loves, a great circle of friends—but her love life is a total disaster. And it's about to get worse. Rescued from the most embarrassing moment of her life by smoking-hot Italian Nico Rossi, she decides to give up on love and settle for sex. But dark, dangerous Nico has his own ideas about what he wants from Hayley…

I hope you have as much fun reading this story as I had writing it.

Find out more about my books on my website, www.sarahmorgan.com, and chat with me on Facebook about books, shoes, life and all things fun and fabulous.

Sarah

xxx

CHAPTER ONE

'DEARLY BELOVED,' THE priest droned, 'we are gathered here today to witness—'

A mistake of massive proportions, I thought gloomily, holding my breath and sitting up straight in a bid to stop my bridesmaid dress splitting at the seams. Any moment now I was going to burst out of this pukey-yellow tube and the wedding would forever be remembered as the one where the bridesmaid exposed herself. Not that I was prudish. Far from it. I'd danced on plenty of tables in my time, but on an ideal day I'd prefer not to find myself revealing *all* Victoria's secrets to Great-Uncle Henry.

Some girls went through their lives dreaming of being a bridesmaid. You heard people talking about it as if it were a life goal. I had a list of life goals. I wanted to build a robot, visit Peru (I've always had a thing about llamas), work for NASA. *Bridesmaid?* That was nowhere on my list.

My parents married when they were both twenty-one. They stood at the front of a church much like this one wearing ridiculous clothes they wouldn't normally be seen dead in, made all the usual promises—have and hold, death us do part, blah, blah—and then divorced when I was eight. Which taught me one thing—that a wedding is just a party by another name.

Because my neck was the only part of me that could move without straining a seam, I turned my head and glanced sideways. Through a forest of fascinators and absurd hats that made me think of UFOs, I could see the door that led to a pretty private churchyard, now covered in a light dusting of snow. I was glad it was pretty because I was sure I was going to be there soon. *Here lies Hayley, who exploded out of her dress at the most inconvenient moment of her short, very unsatisfactory life and promptly died of shame.*

The tiny church was crammed with people and stuffed full of extravagant flower displays, the cloying scent of lilies thickening the air and mingling unpleasantly with the smell of perfume from the elderly aunts. My nose tickled and my head started to throb.

The priest was still droning on in a hypnotic voice

that could have been recorded and sold for millions as a cure for insomnia. 'If anyone knows any reason why these two may not be joined, speak now...'

Any reason?

Was he kidding?

I could have given him at least ten reasons without even revving up a brain cell.

Number one—the groom was a total bastard.

Number two—he'd slept with the bride's sister and at least two of the bride's friends.

Number three—it was three days until Christmas and who the hell was dumb enough to get married when they should have been rushing round buying last-minute presents?

Number four—it was far too cold to be wearing a strapless dress and at this rate I was going to be eating my Christmas dinner in hospital with a nasty bout of pneumonia.

Number five—

'Hayley, are you OK?' My sister Rosie nudged me in the ribs, increasing the strain on my dress.

Of course I wasn't OK. We both knew I wasn't fucking OK. That was why she'd agreed to come with me, but this was hardly the moment for sisterly bonding over margaritas. To be honest, if she'd passed me a margarita I wouldn't have known whether to drink it or drown myself in it.

I was good at statistics and I could tell you right now there was a 99 percent chance this wedding was going to end in tears. Probably mine.

'You should have said no when she asked you to be her bridesmaid,' Rosie hissed. 'It was a mean thing to do when everyone knows you used to date him.'

And there it was. Right there. Reason number five why the bride and groom shouldn't get married. Because he'd once said he wanted to marry me.

I'd told him no. I didn't want to get married. Ever. I'd never had ambitions to be a bridesmaid and I had even fewer to be a bride. I assumed if he loved me, it wouldn't make a difference. I mean, what was the big deal about a wedding ceremony? It wasn't as if it stopped people breaking up. All that mattered was being together, wasn't it?

Apparently not.

Turned out Charles was very traditional. He was climbing the ladder in an investment bank in the city and needed a wife prepared to devote herself to the advancement of his career. I've always been crap on ladders. I tried explaining I was as excited about my own career as he was about his and his response had been to dump me. In a very public way, I might add, just so that no one was under any illusions as to who had done the dumping.

Admittedly it hurt to be dumped, but nowhere near as much as it hurt to admit I'd wasted ten months on a guy who wasn't remotely interested in the real me.

I realised everyone in the church was looking at me accusingly, as if I'd come here on purpose to make things awkward. To somehow punish him for not choosing me.

Look again, I wanted to yell, *and see which one of us is being punished.*

What girl in her right mind would choose to turn up at her ex's wedding dressed in the fashion equivalent of a giant condom?

Was it my fault the bride wanted to make a public declaration about which one of us the groom was marrying? And I knew I wasn't exactly guilt-free in all this. I could have said no. But then everyone would have thought I was moping and broken-hearted and I had my pride.

That was the first thing mum taught us—never let a man know you're broken-hearted. Which might be why our dad didn't stick around for long, but more on that later.

I could feel myself turn pink, which I knew had to look horrible against the pukey yellow. I think the fabric was officially described as 'misty dawn' but if I saw a dawn like that I wouldn't put a foot out of bed.

Worst of all? *He* was looking at me. No, not Charlie—he hadn't once glanced in my direction, the coward. The best man. Charlie's friend from school, although they'd grown apart in recent years and the friend was now a super successful lawyer. To be honest I was a bit surprised he'd agreed to be best man, but Charlie had lost a lot of friends since he'd taken a job in the city and started only hanging out with people who were 'useful' to him.

The best man's name was Niccolò Rossi and he was half Italian. And hot. Seriously hot. In the looks department this man had been gifted by the gods.

Unfortunately immediately after the gods had dished out super clever brain, dark good looks and an incredible body, they obviously decided too much of a good thing was a bad thing and withheld humour. Which was a shame because Nico had an amazing mouth. A perfect sensual curve that would probably look good in a smile. Only he never used it to smile. Never. And he wasn't using it now as he looked at me. He clearly wasn't amused to see me sitting there. I wasn't amused either. It was probably the first time we'd felt the same way about anything. He lived in London. We'd met the same night I met Charlie and although we were always bumping into each other on the social circuit, we'd barely spoken. I knew he wasn't my type. He disapproved of me and I was done with men who disapproved of me. Charlie hated the fact I was an engineer. He always wanted me to wear frilly dresses to compensate. No wonder we came unstuck.

Nico cast me an icy glance at the same moment I looked at him.

Bad timing.

Our eyes clashed. His were a dark, dangerous black and everything inside me turned to liquid.

I glared, taking my anger with myself out on him.

I hated that he made me feel this way. He didn't like me. I didn't like him. We were polar opposites. I was fun-loving, friendly and honest about my feelings. He was zipped up, ruthlessly contained and cold as the inside of my freezer. There had been moments over the past few years when I'd been tempted to leap on him with a blowtorch to see if I could thaw him out.

He'd given me a lift home in his car once when Charlie had been too drunk to walk, let alone drive. It was a night I'd tried to forget. We'd been celebrating my job, which for some reason had sent Charlie over the edge.

Nico drove a red Ferrari, just about the sexiest car on the planet, and he was ruthlessly tidy. There wasn't a single screwed-up piece of paper in sight. No mess (although by the time he dropped me off there may have been traces of saliva where I'd drooled all over his car). His suits were Tom Ford, his shoes polished and his shirts a crisp, pristine white. But underneath that carefully polished appearance there was something raw and elemental that no amount of sophisticated tailoring could conceal.

I'd been wearing my favourite black dress that night and I remember he didn't look at me once. Not even at my legs, which were definitely my best feature, especially when I dressed them up in four-inch stilettos (no pain no gain). He hadn't bothered to hide his disapproval then and he wasn't hiding it now.

His burning gaze lowered to my neckline and that sensual, unsmiling mouth tightened into a line of grim censure.

I wanted to stand up and point out that the dress wasn't my choice. That it was yet another trick on the part of the bride to make sure I looked hideous. Quite honestly my breasts were too big for this dress and breasts generally weren't on the guest list to a wedding. Mine were so big they could have qualified for separate invitations.

Nico Rossi obviously didn't think they should have been invited at all.

Truth? I found him intimidating and I hated that.

I was a modern, independent woman. I'd never worn pink and I'd never had the urge to coo over strange babies in prams. My best subjects at school were Math, Physics and Technology. I was the only girl in the class and I always had better marks than the boys, which usually pissed them off, but I figured that was their problem not mine. I had a degree in aeronautical engineering and was working on a supersecret project to do with satellites. I couldn't tell you more than that or I'd have to kill you and eat you and you didn't need a degree in engineering to know there was no room in this dress for two people. I loved my job. It excited me more than any man I'd ever met. But that could have been because I constantly messed up my love life.

Every. Single. Time.

Honestly, how could an intelligent woman get it so badly wrong? I'd tried to apply data analysis methods to my dating history but failed to extract anything meaningful from the results except that getting it wrong hurt. I always seemed to end up compromising who I was, but that's in the genes. Rosie and I watched our mum contort who she was for men who subsequently left her. As I said, we weren't good at relationships, which was probably why I was sitting here single, watching my ex get married.

I breathed in the smell of this musty old church and thought about all the promises that had been made here only to be broken a few years down the line. And right there and then, I made a decision.

No more feelings.

Feelings just led to misery and I was done with misery.

Not that I'd ever been the sort of girl to wait by the phone, willing it to ring. God, no. If a guy played those games with me, I deleted him from my contacts. But that didn't mean I couldn't be hurt. And frankly, what was the point?

'I've made a New Year's Resolution.' I risked the dress and leaned closer to Rosie. 'And I'm starting right now.'

'You're never wearing pukey-yellow again?' She eyed my dress. 'Good decision.'

I ignored her. 'I'm sick of romantic relationships. Why bother? I can go to the movies with girlfriends. I can chat with girlfriends. I can laugh with girlfriends.'

'That's your New Year's resolution?'

'Everything I need in life I can get from girlfriends,' I hissed, 'apart from one thing—'

Rosie coughed. 'Well, you can—'

'No, I can't. I need a man for that part. But only

that part. From now on I'm using men for sex. Nothing else.'

'Well, as resolutions go, I predict that one is going to be a lot more fun than giving up chocolate.'

I could always rely on my sister for support.

The more I thought about it, the more convinced I was it was a brilliant idea. 'I should have thought of it before.' I was talking out of the corner of my mouth, trying not to attract glares from the elderly aunts. 'Instead of trying to find a man who can make me laugh and is actually interested in me, instead of wondering what I can do for his career, I look for one thing. Sex appeal.'

'If all you're interested in is sex appeal, you could start with Nico Rossi,' Rosie whispered. 'He is scorching hot.'

Not just me then.

The problem was, I didn't want to find Nico sexy. I didn't want to think of him naked or wonder how it would feel to be kissed by him. He didn't like me. It disturbed my sense of order and fairness that I should find him attractive.

I looked away, but not for long.

I couldn't help myself. I sneaked another look. It was some consolation that every other woman under ninety was staring, too. If ever there was such a thing as raw sex appeal, Nico had it. He was the sort of guy that made you think about sin in a big way, which wasn't a good thing when you were sitting in church with your breasts half exposed.

I couldn't wait to get to the bathroom so that I could unzip my dress and give my ribs the freedom they deserved.

When was this wedding going to end?

Enough already.

Just say *I do* and go and live your lives until your realise what you should have said was *I don't.*

But now they were staring into each other's eyes and reciting handwritten personalised messages.

I promise to love you forever and cherish you.

I promise never to cancel your subscription to the sports channel.

(OK I made that one up but you get the point)

I wriggled in my seat, wondering whether Nico Rossi spoke in Italian when he was having sex. He'd brought his younger sister to the wedding—a sleek, dark vision of slender perfection. She was poised and sophisticated, just like him. Every now and then she glanced at him adoringly, as if he were a god. It seemed unnatural to me. I mean, I loved my sister but there were plenty of days I wanted to poke her in the eye. But these were perfect people who would never show emotion in public. They probably never argued. They were the sort who believed marriage to be an exciting journey.

I was always sick on journeys.

Thanks to our parents' less than stellar example, my sister and I were both equally screwed-up about relationships. Not that there weren't men in our lives. Far from it. Men were always attracted by Rosie's sweet, heart-shaped face and her pretty smile. They thought she was fragile and needed protecting. Then they discovered my sister had a black belt in karate and could break a man's bones with one kick and they usually retreated nervously, licking their wounded machismo.

There *was* a guy once, but if I so much as thought his name she'd break my bones, too, so it was a subject I didn't touch.

Just when I thought this wedding was never going to end, the priest benevolently told the groom he could kiss the bride. He'd been kissing the bride and half her friends regularly for the past six months without permission from anyone, but no one seemed to care about that.

I couldn't help wondering if the kiss was for my benefit, to remind me what I'd turned down.

It was very Hollywood. No bumping noses or awkward moments. Scripted. The sort of kiss where you just knew they were thinking about how it looked on the outside, not how it felt on the inside.

There seemed to be an awful lot of tongue involved.

Rosie made sick choking noises next to me.

God, I loved my sister.

And then finally, *finally*, it was over.

I breathed a huge sigh of relief.

And my dress split.

CHAPTER TWO

OH FUCK, SO now I was naked. Not just wearing a condom, but a split condom, and suddenly no one was looking at the bride and groom—they were staring at me and I couldn't exactly blame them because there was plenty to see. There were times when I was happy to be the centre of attention, but this wasn't one of them.

Why oh why hadn't I worn a bra?

I'd tried it, but it had shown through the cheap, shiny fabric, so I'd decided in the interests of vanity that if I *had* to wear this hideous dress at least my outline would be smooth and perfect.

Another bad decision. The dress had split down both side seams simultaneously, exposing me completely from the waist up. I felt like a half-peeled banana, but

I probably looked like one of those women who turned up at stag parties and leapt out of cakes.

I was strip-o-gram bridesmaid.

Everyone was staring, transfixed by delicious horror, all deeply relieved it hadn't happened to them. But it could never have happened to them. Only to me. My life had a habit of unraveling, only usually not quite as literally as this.

The snow and the draughty, under-heated old church had conspired to make my nipples stand to attention. I tried to cover them with my hands, but then I realised I was probably making it worse. Now I wasn't just naked—I was touching myself.

For the first time in quite a few years, I prayed.

Kill me now.

Mum had always drummed into Rosie and me that we should wear clean underwear in case of an accident, although to be fair I don't think this was the sort of accident she had in mind when she dished out that advice. I wished I'd listened, but I honestly hadn't thought my underwear, or lack of it, was going to be an issue. Every unattached girl hoped she would score at a wedding, but I was a realist. No man was going to hit on a woman wearing a giant body condom. Don't misunderstand me—I was all for safe sex. I insisted on condoms. It was just that I didn't usually try and squeeze my whole self into one.

The dress was a horribly tight tube, floor length, which basically meant my legs were locked together. I couldn't even run away. I was like a mermaid, but without an ocean to drown in. Escape would be a slow, shuffling, breast-bouncing affair.

Scarlet-faced, I tried to grab the misbehaving fabric and cover myself with that, but honestly it was like trying to cover Big Ben with a handkerchief.

Somewhere through the swirling clouds of embarrassment I heard Rosie snort. She was laughing so hard I knew she was going to be as much use to me as a non-alcoholic cocktail at a party. Rosie had a problem with laughter. She couldn't control it. Watching her laugh usually made me laugh, too, but any desire to laugh was squashed by the look in ruthless Nico Rossi's eyes.

While everyone else was gaping in horrified silence (and I can tell you they weren't looking at my face) he strode across the aisle towards me, all broad shouldered and powerful like a warrior preparing to repel an invading army.

I waited for Rosie to leap to her feet and execute one of her incredible scissor kicks that would flatten him, but my useless sister was doubled up with tears pouring down her face and Nico was still striding. I guessed it would take a lot to flatten a man like him.

Just for a moment I shivered because whatever he lacked in the emotional warmth department, physically he was truly spectacular—stomach-melting, willpower-destroying spectacular. The sort of man you couldn't look at without thinking about sex.

Dark, glittering eyes were focused on me like a laser-guided weapon programmed to destroy.

His role as best man was to support the groom and solve problems and right now I was the problem. Or at least, my breasts were. They were loose and free and I could tell from the look on his face he thought breasts like mine shouldn't be allowed out without a permit.

The elderly aunts had their eyes averted, but the elderly uncles were staring at me, their bulging eyes reminding me of sea creatures. I saw sweat on their brows and was just wondering whether I was going to be responsible for adding more bodies to that pretty churchyard when Nico reached me. He removed his jacket in a smooth movement that made me think he'd be good at undressing women, and wrapped it around my shoulders. Actually 'wrapped' was too gentle a word for what he did, but either way my bouncing breasts were now safely buried under Tom Ford. His jacket felt warm. It smelled delicious. It smelled of *him*.

'Move!' It was a command, not a request and I opened my mouth to point out my legs were tied together, but his hand was on my back and he was propelling me down the aisle. *Down the aisle.* That's right, I, Hayley Miller of 42 Cherry Tree Crescent, Notting Hill, was shuffling down the aisle with a man, something I always said I'd never do, except that I was doing it backwards and half-naked, so it probably didn't count.

I staggered past a sea of faces, all with their mouths hanging open. They reminded me of a nest of baby birds waiting to be fed and I wasn't just feeding them morsels of gossip—I'd given them a banquet. At least they wouldn't need to eat at the reception.

And behind the fascinated horror was the delight some people felt when they witnessed someone else's public humiliation. They'd be talking about this moment for weeks. Who was I kidding? Years. One thing I knew for sure—I was never trusting a condom again.

But I had more immediate problems to worry about.

I had no idea where we were going.

This was a small private church in the grounds of a stately home. England was full of that sort of thing and, since the credit crunch, even the very rich were looking for ways to supplement their income. Hiring out the dusty family chapel for weddings was a clever way of allowing less privileged folk to pretend for that one day of their lives that they actually lived like this. I didn't think it was any more fake than exchanging vows and promises about loving each other forever and then splitting up a few years later. In other words, none of it meant anything, so why not go over the top? If dressing like an over-whipped dessert made you happy, then go for it I say (but for God's sake get one that fits).

Everyone wanted to get married in this particular chapel, not for religious reasons but because the door was pretty and looked good in the photos.

'Oh, God, the photos! What about the photos?' I stopped dead, but he pushed me forward into a room and slammed the door.

It was just the two of us and the silence was really loud.

I looked around me and saw we were in a room with wood paneling and portraits of unsmiling dukes on unsmiling horses. In the corner was a perfectly deco-rated Christmas tree. No wonky home-made decora-tions like the ones Rosie and I used in our apartment, but designer perfection.

I was pretty sure we weren't supposed to be here, but I guessed Nico wasn't giving much thought to protect-ing the assets of our hosts. He was more interested in hiding *my* assets from the gawping guests.

What was I supposed to say?

What was the etiquette for a serious wardrobe malfunction?

I had a feeling 'oops' wasn't going to cut it and asking for a needle and thread would have been like asking for a teacup to bail out the Titanic.

'Er—nice jacket.' And because I was wearing his jacket, he was in his shirtsleeves and I could see the swell of hard male muscle pressing against the fabric. His shirt was pristine white and I noticed his skin was golden, not pale and pasty like Charlie's, and his jaw had the beginnings of a dark shadow. Thick, dark lashes framed eyes that were indecently sexy—the only thing that spoiled it was the dangerous glint of anger.

He dragged his fingers through hair that was usually smooth and sleek, exploded into Italian, and then switched language in midsentence as if realising that if he wanted to insult me he'd better do it in a language I understood. '*Cristo*, what were you thinking choosing a dress that revealing?'

'I didn't choose it.'

'Then you should have refused to wear it.' His gaze was fixed on mine and didn't waver.

Clearly he'd had no desire to ogle my bare breasts. I told myself that didn't bother me.

What *did* bother me was the unconcealed look of disapproval on his handsome face.

I was sure he was a very successful lawyer. I didn't even know which bit of the law he dealt with, but whatever he did I was sure he was the best of the best. I knew that if I were on the witness stand and he fixed me with that penetrating gaze I would have confessed to pretty much anything.

Yes, Your Honour, it's true that on the twenty-second day of December I wore a giant condom to a wedding... No, I had no idea I would be arrested for antisocial behavior—condoms are supposed to only have a 2 percent failure rate, but in my case it was 150 percent. Yes, I understand there were serious consequences. Wedding interruptus.

I wondered why he was so angry.

It wasn't as if the groom had ended up with me. This episode could have just been labeled 'narrow escape'.

Outrage started to simmer inside me. I was the victim of a cruel fashion crime, blameless in everything except my proportions and I wasn't about to apologise for my breasts.

And anyway, I felt a bit funny inside. Not queasy exactly, but a bit dizzy and swimmy-headed. I thought it was probably hearing him speaking Italian. The only Italian I knew I learned from a menu and there was nothing sexy about *Pizza Margherita* even if you tried saying it in a sultry voice.

This man, however, was spectacularly sexy and everything that came out of his mouth made me want to grab him and do very, *very* bad things which was definitely off limits because Nico was the sort who was always ruthlessly in control of himself and behaved impeccably in public. I assumed lawyers weren't allowed to misbehave.

'Why the fuck *are* you here, Hayley? You are the master of bad decisions.' He spoke through his teeth as if he were afraid that if he opened his mouth a tirade of insults would escape.

Frankly I was surprised to hear him say 'fuck'.

But now he'd said it, I started thinking about it. Not the word, but the act. I couldn't help it. Truthfully I'd been thinking about it long before he'd said that word. I doubted any woman could look at Nico and *not* think of it. Not love or romance, you understand. He wasn't the hearts and roses sort of man. I couldn't imagine him risking his suit by changing a nappy or rolling up his perfectly ironed sleeves to wash a greasy saucepan, but sex? God, yes. All it took was one look to know this man would know everything there was to know about hard, hot, sweaty sex.

For a wild moment I wanted to ask if he'd impart

some of his knowledge, but then I remembered he'd just told me I made bad decisions. There was only so much abuse a girl could take in one day and I was right up to my limit. When you work in a male-dominated profession as I do, you're used to being judged. Most of the time I let it wash over me. If I threatened their masculinity that was their problem, not mine. Occasionally I fought back. Sometimes I took sadistic pleasure in surprising people, but I was damned if I'd allow myself to be told I made bad decisions by a man who never let himself go.

I stood up straighter and pushed my chest out (good job I was wearing his jacket). 'Excuse *me*, but what gives you the right to judge my decisions?'

'We could start with the fact you're currently naked from the waist up under my jacket. Fix the dress. I'm the best man. I have duties to perform.'

And I was willing to bet he'd perform them well.

Oh, God, I had to stop thinking like that.

'The dress is unfixable. And I couldn't refuse to wear it. This was what Cressida wanted.'

'Your half-naked body on display? I don't think so.' He threw me a look that would have terrified an entire army into immediate surrender. 'But you're just a girl who can't say no.'

'What's that supposed to mean?' I exploded, which

considering I was half-naked wasn't a good idea. Because I was quite physical I tended to add emphasis to what I was saying by using my hands. Up until a moment ago my hands had been holding the front of his jacket together. Now they were waving around wildly, preparing to act in my defense. Unfortunately they were not the only part of me to be waving around wildly.

His eyes darkened and I realised that he had stopped looking at my face.

Suddenly there were four of us in the room.

Me, him and my breasts.

I saw a tiny muscle move in his jaw and then his gaze lifted to mine and that was the moment I discovered that looking at someone could make you burn inside.

'I can say no.' My voice came out croaky and I realised the timing of that sentence wasn't great because I knew, I just knew, that both of us were thinking about sex.

'What the hell are you doing here, Hayley? At this wedding? Have you no pride?'

'Pride is the reason I'm here. If I'd stayed away everyone would have thought I was broken-hearted.'

'And are you?' His question surprised me as much as the roughness of his voice.

We didn't exactly have the sort of relationship that

included an exchange of confidences and that was a deeply personal question. I had no intention of answering it.

I hadn't even told Rosie how bad I felt, although she knew of course. That was why she was here. Solidarity even in the absence of confession. That was one of the unspoken rules of true sisterhood.

The second was that we were going to leave at the first possible moment, scoot back to our apartment in London and drown the memories of today in a large bottle of wine while we wrapped presents and finished decorating our apartment for Christmas.

Not that I was broken-hearted about Charlie—I wasn't. It was more the misery of being forced to confront yet more evidence of how utterly impossible relationships were.

I was mourning the fairy tale, which was ridiculous when I thought about it because I'd never believed in the fairy tale.

'Hayley? *Cristo*, answer the question.' His voice was raw and thickened by an emotion I didn't recognise. I assumed it was anger, since that was the only emotion he ever seemed to feel around me. 'Are you broken-hearted?'

The question hung between us in an atmosphere that was heavy and sweaty. A moment ago I'd been freezing. Someone needed to open a window. It was stifling in here.

'Unless you're a cardiologist, the condition of my heart is none of your business.' I might have been hiding my feelings but I wasn't hiding anything else. I lifted my hands to close my jacket but he was there before me. Strong male fingers tangled with mine and the backs of his fingers brushed against my breasts. His hands were warm and chemistry shot through me. It was like falling on an electric fence.

Both of us froze.

The only sound in the room was his breathing. Or maybe it was my breathing.

He was standing really close to me, so close I had a magnified view of hot masculinity. My eyes were level with that darkened jaw, that unsmiling mouth and those incredible *bed me if you're lucky* eyes.

Right at the moment I so, *so* wanted to get that lucky.

I knew he wouldn't be good for me. He'd probably be a bit like junk food—something you could crave even while knowing it had no nutritional value and might make you feel sick later.

I didn't care about the wedding. I didn't care that I'd be gossiped about for the next two decades. All I wanted was to feel that mouth on mine and find out whether kissing him would be as good as I thought it would.

Oh, God, why not?

Today had been such a total disaster I might as well try and extract one decent memory to comfort me in the hours of cringing flashbacks that were bound to follow.

Telling myself I was doing us both a favor, I grabbed the front of his shirt and was about to pull him towards me when he muttered something in Italian and dragged me towards him by the lapels of his jacket.

We collided, locked together like wild animals in the mating season.

CHAPTER THREE

BODIES, MOUTHS, EVERY part of us that could touch were touching, and although I had no idea who made the first move I didn't care any more because his mouth was warm and skilled and his kiss confirmed what I'd already suspected—

That he was the hottest man on the face of the earth.

Whatever else it was, this wasn't a scripted kiss.

I doubted either of us would have known or cared if anyone else was watching. We were so wrapped up in each other, so absorbed in the moment, we wouldn't have noticed if a horse had leapt from one of the paintings and started galloping around the room.

I felt the erotic slide of his tongue in my mouth and moaned aloud because what he was doing connected a million tiny circuits inside me and set off a chain reaction until I was fairly sure my body was close to melt-down. I didn't care that he never smiled because I knew now his mouth was made for kissing and he proved it with every delicious, skilled stroke of his tongue. My arms were round his neck, my body pressed against his—and his was hard, muscular and just about perfect. Under that shockingly expensive suit, the man was ripped. Everything was ripped. My dress, his body and my reputation.

I couldn't help myself. I covered the front of his trousers with the flat of my hand and felt him, hard and thick against my palm.

'*Cristo*—' he muttered against my lips and slammed me back against the wall, his mouth hot and demanding on mine. His hands had moved from the jacket to my breasts and I felt a thrill of delicious excitement as his thumbs grazed my nipples.

Usually I closed my eyes when I kissed, but not this time.

His eyes were fixed on mine, dark with heat and raw desire. It was the sexiest experience of my life and I didn't want to miss a single moment of it.

My mind wasn't capable of much coherent thought, but I knew I'd been wrong about one thing—

Nico Rossi wasn't a good boy. He was a bad boy dressed in a good suit.

Heat pulsed between us, the chemistry screaming, scorching and intense. His fingers drove into my hair, which tumbled out of its clip and slid over his hand. His mouth was pressing hot, sensual kisses against my neck and lower.

He murmured something in Italian and I was about to ask him to translate when I realised I didn't want him to. Knowing what he was saying might spoil everything. There was no way I was ever going to understand what was going on here anyway, so what was the point in trying?

I felt the thrust of his hard thigh between mine and there was another ripping sound as the seams tore a bit further. If the bridesmaid dress hadn't already been ruined it would have been now. I didn't think he even noticed. His mouth devoured mine and he yanked what was left of the stupid dress up and locked his hands on my shifting hips.

I strained against him, feeling the hard thrust of him against me and then I felt his hand move to my inner thigh. The anticipation almost killed me, and then he was stroking me with those long, knowing fingers, somehow programmed to touch me in exactly the right place even though I hadn't said a word or made a sound. My mouth was on his, we were breathing the same air, biting, licking and it was the most erotic thing I've ever experienced. I wasn't thinking about anything except how good it felt and then he slid his fingers inside me and good became incredible and I could feel myself pulse around him. I was gripping his shoulder because my knees were so weak I thought I might slide to the floor if I wasn't holding on, but that left me with one hand free and I wasn't going to waste it.

I wrapped my hand around him and felt him thicken in my grasp. As I stroked him I heard him growl deep in his throat and it was the sexiest sound I'd ever heard, even sexier because I knew I was the one who had done that to him. This man who was so big on control was *losing* control, and he was losing it because of me.

His fingers were skilled, finding that exact spot with unerring accuracy and I felt the first flutters of orgasm.

We'd barely exchanged a word before today, this man and I, and yet here we were locked in this un-imaginable intimacy. His knee nudged my thighs fur-ther apart, giving him full access and he kept using his fingers, kept kissing me until I felt everything inside me tighten and pulse. I was close, *so close*, and he knew because he was right there with me, his fingers con-trolling everything I was feeling, his mouth breathing in my gasps.

'Come,' he ordered softly, and normally I was very bad at doing what I was told but this time our objectives were clearly aligned and I tightened my hand around the glorious thickness of him and then heard someone calling my name.

'Hayley?' It was my sister, using one of her frantic stage whispers, knocking on doors as she searched for me. Presumably she'd finally stopped laughing for long enough to work out I might be in trouble.

Shit.

Nico and I stared at each other, eyes and mouths still locked together. My body was suspended in a state of intense excitement.

For once in my life I wished Rosie had just carried on laughing and not tried to help me out.

Here I was, hovering on the edge of what I knew was going to be the best orgasm of my life with the hottest man I was ever going to meet and my sister was banging on the door.

I was going to kill her. Slowly. If I was going to die in agony then I was going to make sure she did, too.

'Hayley? Are you OK?'

It was a measure of how turned on I was that having my sister banging on the door hadn't made any difference to the way I felt.

Nico swore against my mouth (in both Italian and English, in case you were wondering), and I was just about to ask whether he'd locked the door when it burst open.

Fortunately Nico had his back to our audience, shielding me. I had yet another reason to be thankful for those broad, muscular shoulders.

With admirable calm, he removed his fingers and his mouth from my body and somehow managed to pull my dress down and draw the lapels of his jacket together at the same time. He was impressive in a crisis—smooth and composed. Rosie had seen most of it before, of course. We'd lived together since we left home to go to college and we didn't lock doors very often, so at this point I was more exasperated than embarrassed.

But then I looked past his shoulders (and that took some willpower, I can tell you, because it was the best view I'd seen in a long time) and saw a shocked face that didn't belong to my sister.

Nico's sister was staring at him as if she'd never seen him before.

Oh crappity, crap, crap.

Her eyes were wide and shocked, her mouth slightly agape.

She obviously thought I'd corrupted her usually controlled brother. And maybe I had. I was certainly well on my way. From the moment he'd touched me, I'd thought about nothing but him. And before you judge me I can tell you without a flicker of doubt that if this man had kissed you, you wouldn't have been thinking of anything but him either.

He swore under his breath. 'Go back to the church, Kiara.' It was a command, and she colored and stepped back without question.

If he'd spoken to me like that I would have posted his Tom Ford suit to a worthy charity, but she didn't say a word. Just obeyed him like a puppy in an obedience class.

I decided it must be the shock that had stopped her from standing up for herself. And I was responsible for that shock.

So much for having a sexual relationship without emotional involvement. It seemed that no matter what rules you played by, *someone* always got hurt.

I wanted to tell her not to worry, that we hated each other really, but she'd already gone and I was left with more than a split dress to worry about.

I'd thought my embarrassment couldn't get any deeper.

Turned out I'd been wrong about that, too.

CHAPTER FOUR

'BEST WEDDING *EVER*.' It was Christmas Eve and Rosie was stretching on the living room floor, surrounded by half-wrapped Christmas presents. She spent a lot of time stretching. I'd learned to give her a wide berth because there had been more than one occasion when I'd moved too close and ended up with her foot in my face. She'd started karate at the age of six, then she'd added in Muay Thai when she was eighteen and met— But I wasn't allowed to mention him. Let's just say we call him He Who Shall Not Be Named (and he's not that Voldemort guy from Harry Potter, although from the smile on my sister's face at the time I think he might have had a magic wand hidden somewhere).

'Glad you were entertained.'

Snow drifted lazily past the windows. The streets

of London were white and everyone was wrapped up against the cold in bright scarves and outrageous hats. That was one of the many things I loved about living in London. People weren't afraid to dress creatively, especially where we lived. In Notting Hill we were surrounded by artists, musicians and writers. And my angel-faced, karate-loving, kick-boxing sister.

I snuggled deeper into the sofa, my laptop balanced on my thighs because I couldn't be bothered to walk to the table and anyway, it saved on heating bills. 'Can we stop talking about the wedding?'

She'd been laughing non-stop for the past three days.

Sisterly love was wearing thin.

I pretended to be absorbed by my laptop, but if I was honest I'd barely done any work since we'd arrived home from the wedding. I couldn't concentrate. My brain was jammed up with the hottest memory of my life. I couldn't stop thinking about it. About *him*. Mostly about the way Mr Super Cool had gone from ignoring me to virtually having sex with me. The change in him had been shocking and, well, exciting. What wasn't so exciting was the fact it had been interrupted and there was no chance of a repeat performance, which basically meant I was doomed to die of sexual frustration. Not that I hadn't tried to do something about that, but no vibrator was ever going

to come close to the unique bedroom talents of Nico
Rossi. It was like watching a boxed set, ending an episode on a cliffhanger and then realising you'd lost the
final DVD. I desperately wanted to know what happened next.

But I was never going to because Nico hadn't liked
me before the wedding, so he was going to like me
even less since I ruined the day and walked off with
his Tom Ford.

For a couple of days I'd nurtured a fantasy he might
contact me, but of course he hadn't. Real life is a split
dress and embarrassment, not a hot guy ringing you.

I answered another email, trying to block out the
memory of the wedding. I'd scoured YouTube for days,
checking that no one had uploaded a video of my diz-
zying descent into ignominy. So far all seemed well,
but if I could have dug a hole and lived underground
for a while, I would have done. 'Why the hell did you
have to walk in when you did?'

'Why the hell didn't you lock the door if you were
planning to have sex? I've wrapped a load of "spare"
presents by the way. They're the ones without labels.'
She spun and kicked, almost removing a lamp from
the table. If the lamp had been a person, it would have
been unconscious. And she wondered why men were

intimidated by her. Sex with my sister could probably have been classified as a lethal sport.

And talking of sex…

'We weren't having sex!' I watched as Rosie paused to arrange the presents in a pile under the perfectly shaped fir tree we'd picked up from the garden centre. I would have had a fake one, but she said we had so much fake in our life growing up, we deserved the real thing. Personally I didn't see anything romantic about picking dried green needles out of the bottom of your feet in March, but that was just me. 'Haven't you overdone the "spare" presents this year?'

My sister always bought extra Christmas presents. She said it was because it made the tree look festive, but I knew her idea of a terrible Christmas would be for someone to turn up and her not have a gift for them. She was very generous—it was all linked with her fairy-tale view of the world. Not that she was idealistic, but she believed you could make your own fairy tale if you worked hard enough at it. Who needed a prince when you had a credit card and online shopping? When we were little she was the one who danced around the room in pink tights with a tiara on her head, pretending to be a princess. Then our parents split up and she decided she'd rather be the Karate Kid.

My sister's most important self-created fairy tale was

Christmas. Because we'd never had a proper family Christmas, she overcompensated madly. Hence the tree, the stockings and her determination that no one we knew would spend the day alone.

'I'm going to pick up the turkey.' She spun and executed another kick and her blonde hair flew around her face. There were times when I thought she should have auditioned to play Bond (and I do mean Bond, not the dopey girl planted in the film so he can have sex). She trained for hours every day, but it had paid off and she'd landed a great job coaching martial arts at Fit and Physical in the City. She was also building a list of clients for personal training. Her results were startling, but I guessed that was because they were all terrified of my sweet-faced sister. If you didn't put in the effort she kicked your butt. Literally.

Another ten emails pinged into my inbox. We were in the middle of this huge project at work and it wasn't going away just because most of London had shut down for the holidays.

Half of me was hoping one of those emails was from Nico. I didn't need to tell you which half but let's put it this way—I was wondering if it was too late to ask Santa for a new vibrator. Was there one called The Niccolò? That was the one I wanted.

Idly I typed 'vibrator—the Niccolò' into the search engine. 'I have to send the jacket back.'

'You can't do it today—he won't be in the office. It's Christmas Eve and it's snowing.' Rosie grabbed her coat. 'Come with me. Better than moping.'

'I'm not moping.'

'You're moping. And dreaming in Italian.'

I closed the lid of my laptop so she couldn't see what I'd just typed. I had *some* secrets. 'If it weren't for you I wouldn't have had to dream. I would have had reality. I would have put my New Year's resolution of emotionless sex into practice.'

'It would have been a waste to rush something so good with a man that hot.'

'So instead I didn't get to do it at all? How is that better?' I ducked as she threw me my coat. 'I'm not going out. I still haven't recovered from being naked in church. Someone might recognise me.'

'The advantage of being naked from the waist up is that no one was looking at your face.' Rosie threw my scarf. 'Unless what you're working on is an emergency, you're coming.'

I wished she hadn't used those exact words.

I wasn't coming. That was the point. And yes, it was close to an emergency. At this rate I'd need resuscitation. Mouth-to-mouth. And mouth to— Well, you get the point. All I could think of was sex, which wasn't good when there was no immediate hope for a satisfactory resolution.

Maybe freezing cold and snow would reduce the need for a vibrator.

It didn't, but I had to admit there was something uplifting about walking through Notting Hill on Christmas Eve. Shop windows sparkled with lights and decorations and everyone was smiling, which didn't make sense when you thought about the number of people who found this a miserable time of year or didn't celebrate, but maybe they'd all stayed indoors.

A family strolled past, dragging an enormous tree. They were all holding hands. A mother, father and two very excited children with pink cheeks and shiny expressions. Something twisted inside me. I didn't understand how I could envy that when it wasn't what I wanted.

I caught Rosie's eye and she shrugged, reading my mind.

That was one of the things I loved about my sister. Not only did she know what I was thinking without me saying it, but the past was the past. If something was messed up, then she was going to make sure she did it differently in the future. She was all about moving forward.

Snow was falling on her hair and I thought how pretty she was. Dancer-slim with amazing green eyes and blonde hair that licked around her face and fell to her shoulders. Long, slim limbs that could knock you out with one kick. It was her superpower.

Everyone else was thinking about Christmas, but I was thinking about the wedding. 'Do you think I ruined their big day?'

'No, but it would serve them right if you did. It was mean of them to insist you be a bridesmaid. Not that he was right for you, but they never should have put you in that position.'

She was my sister. It was her job to try and make me feel better, but I really wanted to believe her. It was Christmas Eve and no one wanted to feel bad about themselves on Christmas Eve.

'It's kind of ironic that I went because of my pride, and ended up half-naked in public and then kissing a man who hates me.'

Rosie made a snorting sound. 'He doesn't hate you. The two of you have chemistry. You always have. You two have always been much better suited than you and Charlie.'

I stopped dead and gaped at her. 'How can you say that?' I analyzed the evidence. 'Nico Rossi has barely ever spoken to me. Whenever we're in the same room, he ignores me. He doesn't like me.' Which made the whole thing all the more confusing. How could I possibly have had such a hot encounter with a man who didn't like me?

'He arranged for a car to drive us home from the wedding so you didn't have to face the guests. That must have cost him a fortune.'

And I'd already tucked the money into the pocket of his Tom Ford. I didn't want to be in debt to Nico. 'He did it because he wanted to get us out of there. I'd already ruined the wedding.'

'He rescued you when everyone else stood around gawping.' My sister had stopped, too. Snow settled on her blonde hair. 'He gave you his jacket. He didn't have to do that.'

I frowned. 'He didn't want me naked in a church.'

My sister bent gracefully and scooped up a handful of snow, forming it into a snowball. 'Who gave you a lift home the night you invited a load of us to celebrate your new job and Charlie proceeded to ignore you and get wasted?'

'Nico.' That evening had been the beginning of the end for Charlie and me. He'd proposed the day after, as an alternative to taking the job. I'd thought he was still drunk and kidding. Turned out he was sober and dead serious. He saw marriage to him as a preferable career option. 'Nico, but he was driving past my house anyway.'

I waited for her to say 'yes, you're right', but instead she watched me steadily and suddenly I wondered what explanation Nico had given his sister. Maybe he'd told her it hadn't been his fault, that he'd been assaulted by my bare breasts and had merely been defending himself. He was a lawyer. I was pretty sure he could plead self-defense better than anyone.

On the other hand he didn't strike me as the sort of man who made excuses.

Take him or leave him.

I'd tried to take him and look where that had got me.

I slid my arm through Rosie's and resolved to stop thinking about him. 'Let's talk about something else.' I'd never spent so long thinking about a man I wasn't even in a relationship with. 'So far my resolution to have emotionless sex isn't turning out so well. Maybe I should have just gone for something more traditional like losing weight and getting fit.'

'You're already fit, and you're not supposed to start your resolution until the New Year. Perhaps you'll meet someone cute tomorrow.' Something in the way she said it made me turn my head suspiciously.

'Who have you invited? Please don't tell me it's that journalist guy.'

'Just all our usual friends and a few others.' She was studying a gingerbread house in the window of our favorite bakery. 'Should we buy that?'

'If you buy any more food there won't be room for the guests. Rosie, who exactly is coming tomorrow?'

'I never know until they knock on the door. You know what it's like—not everyone confirms.' She didn't look at me. The year before she'd invited an entire class from her gym. They were all kicking in our living room.

We wandered on, staring in windows. I thought how much I loved London. We lived in a great area, with shops, markets and lively restaurants on our doorsteps. Our apartment was on the top floor of a beautiful red-brick Victorian house in the trendy part of Notting Hill. The streets were really pretty here and we were round the corner from Portobello market and an easy walk from Kensington Gardens. Loads of our friends lived nearby.

I wondered where Nico lived. Had he gone home to Italy for Christmas?

I hoped he didn't need his jacket.

'Hey, wake up. It's been snowing all night.'

I burrowed under the covers, resenting my sister's energy levels. 'It's too early.'

'It's Christmas. We have to open our stockings and there's loads to do.'

'Only because you insist on inviting half the world to lunch.' I emerged from under the covers and looked out of my attic window.

London was covered in another deep coating of sparkling snow. It almost *was* a fairy tale, except I had to get up and cook Christmas lunch for a bunch of people I'd probably never met before when all I wanted to do was lie in a heap, watch back-to-back TV and try to forget about the disastrous wedding.

Rosie sprang onto the bed and crossed her legs, her daisy pajamas a cheerful, springlike rebellion against the winter weather. 'Do you mind? Would you rather I didn't do this?'

I was about to confess that one year it might be nice to just eat turkey sandwiches and flop in front of the TV when I saw the look of excitement in her eyes and knew I would never, ever, stop her doing this. And anyway, I understood why she did it. We couldn't have a proper 'family Christmas' so she had a 'friend Christmas' instead.

Rosie was determined to create the life she wanted to live and I admired that.

'I think it's great.' And I did. Because of my sister, no one we knew spent Christmas on their own. Everyone with nowhere to go was invited, which meant that some years our apartment was pretty crowded, but I didn't really have a problem with that.

'Are you sure?' She dragged the stockings onto the bed. 'I wondered whether you wouldn't rather just have a quiet day.'

'Not in a million years.'

Don't get me wrong—my sister and I fought, but it was always over the small things. When it was anything to do with our past, we were a united front.

We opened the 'stockings' we'd laid out the night before (she filled mine and I filled hers. Last year we'd bumped heads stuffing stockings at the same time). Each was full of funny low-priced gifts. Thanks to the stress of the wedding, I'd bought all mine on the internet. I had no idea when Rosie had done her shopping. Soon my bed was covered in ripped paper and in amongst chocolates, a notebook, an exceptionally cute stuffed llama, and a festive bra and panty set in red with white faux fur trim, there was a packet of condoms with 'not to be used until the New Year' on them.

I raised an eyebrow. 'I don't remember mentioning those when I wrote to Santa.'

'He knows you've been a good girl this year but he also knows you're going to be a bad girl very soon.' She winked at me. 'And he wants you to be prepared.'

Rosie was as subtle as a kick in the stomach from a reindeer.

I was pretty pleased with the presents I'd chosen for her, and as well as the small things I gave her my main gift—a leather handbag in a soft shade of cappuccino she'd admired in the market back in November.

'I love it.' She cooed over it and then threw me an enigmatic look. 'Your big present is coming later.'

I wondered how my present could be coming later when there were no deliveries on Christmas Day, but I had no time to dwell on it because we were expecting a load of people and we had to produce food.

Surrendering to the inevitable cooking marathon, I showered quickly and teamed my favorite skinny jeans with thigh-length boots and a cute shirt with shell buttons. Underneath I was wearing my new festive underwear (including the bra, in case you were wondering. Never let it be said I don't learn from my mistakes).

I reported for duty in the kitchen just as Rosie staggered through the door carrying the turkey. It had spent the night in our hallway, apparently reaching 'room temperature'.

'This needs a bit of attention. Can you do that while I make the stuffing?'

I looked at it doubtfully because I wasn't much of a cook. 'What sort of attention?'

'There are some stray feathers. Pluck them out.'

She wanted me to pluck the turkey?

'Poultry hair removal isn't exactly my specialty,' I began, but I was talking to myself. Rosie had already left the room, whirling through the flat singing Christmas carols. I wouldn't have minded, but my sister was a much better dancer than she was a singer.

I stared gloomily at the turkey. It had dark stubble on one leg. Clearly the person who had prepared this turkey for the oven had been anxious to leave work early. I looked at the stubby ends poking out of the plump pale skin and sympathised. It wasn't easy keeping yourself smooth. What the hell was I supposed to do?

I pulled my phone out of my pocket and checked my texts and emails but there was still nothing from Nico. Not that I was expecting 'Merry Christmas', but I thought he might at least have demanded his jacket back.

'Stop looking at your phone.' Rosie was back in the kitchen, squeezing orange juice into a bowl of cranberries. 'He isn't going to call you.'

'I have no idea what you mean. I was checking my work emails.'

'On Christmas Day?'

I wondered why she was so sure he wouldn't call me. I had his jacket. It was Tom Ford. If nothing else, he should want it back. A guy like him was bound to be going to lots of smart dinners over the holidays. 'This project is important. And you'll be busy once Christmas is over.' Rosie's phone never stopped ringing with people wanting her to help them get into shape. Usually I didn't see her until February when everyone went back to being inactive slobs.

The doorbell rang. We were nowhere near ready for guests and I looked at her in horror but Rosie smiled, which I thought was a very odd reaction. Given the hairy turkey and the state of our kitchen I would have anticipated screaming.

She vanished to answer the door and I decided life was too short to pluck a turkey. And anyway, I needed rapid results.

I formulated a plan, congratulating myself on my ingenuity. Behind me I could hear our apartment slowly filling up with people and it was quite a few minutes before Rosie came back into our pretty country-style kitchen. 'Hayley, you need to—' She broke off and stared at me in disbelief. 'You're *waxing* the turkey?'

'You told me to remove the stray feathers.' I ripped the strip, removing feathers and most of the skin. 'Oops. That wasn't the way it was supposed to turn out.'

'You were *supposed* to pluck it!'

'There was no time to pluck each feather individually.' We both stared at the skinless leg of the turkey, me with morbid fascination and Rosie with horror.

'I can't believe you waxed our turkey! You've ruined it.'

I felt a stab of guilt. 'Just one leg. And leg meat is often dry.'

'I'm never letting you near my kitchen again.' Rosie shoved me aside and it was only then I remembered she'd come in to tell me something.

'You were telling me I needed to do something. What?' I turned my head and almost passed out because Nico was standing there, his broad shoulders blocking my view of the living room and the other guests.

I'd thought about nothing but him for the past few days. Sometimes when you fantasised about a guy and then you saw him again, you realised you'd built him up in your head. Not Nico. He was truly spectacular. And imposing. He filled the doorway of our kitchen and he glanced from me to the turkey and lifted an eyebrow.

Seriously unbalanced by his unexpected appearance, I gave what I hoped passed for a casual shrug. 'Not everyone likes leg.'

'True.' Those dark eyes met mine with sardonic humor. Not a smile, but definitely humor. 'I'm more of a breast man myself.'

Oh, God, why did he have to say that?

Immediately I was back in that room at the wedding, with him showing me just how much of a breast man he was. I wondered what the hell he was doing here.

Presumably he needed his jacket for some Christmas gathering or other, but this seemed like an odd time to show up on our doorstep.

I turned to look at Rosie, but she was in a panic over the waxed turkey.

My sister had no sense of priorities.

I was about to fetch Nico's jacket and send him on his way when I realised he wasn't alone.

Kiara stood in the doorway, groomed and polished as ever. She gave me an awkward smile, which I returned. At a guess I'd say mine was more awkward than hers. I felt more naked than the turkey (although without being vain, I'd say my legs were looking a hell of a lot better).

Nico was leaning casually against the doorframe watching me from under those thick lashes, the way he had when we'd kissed. He might as well have been touching me because I could feel his gaze right through me. The sensation started as a tingling on the surface of my skin and then it was a warmth through my veins, and then the warmth turned to heat. The heat pooled low in my pelvis and I didn't think it had anything to do with my fur-trimmed panties. It exasperated me that I could feel like this. And what was even more exasperating was the fact he *knew* I was feeling like this. Not that he looked smug or anything. Oh, no. If I'd had to describe his expression I would have said 'watchful'.

He kept looking at me. Unflinching. Unembarrassed. As if he'd asked himself a question and was now looking at the answer.

Then he glanced from me to the woman standing quietly next to him.

'You haven't been formally introduced, have you?'

Oh, great. He was going to ram home the fact that his sister had only ever seen me half-naked. 'No.' I spoke between my teeth. 'We haven't.'

'This is Kiara. Kiara, this is Hayley. You saw her briefly at the wedding.'

All right, enough!

It might have been brief, but I had a feeling it had been fairly comprehensive.

What was the guy playing at? One more comment like that and I'd give him one of my own kicks, which might not have been as impressive or elegant as my sister's, but would still have threatened his ability to father children.

'Hi, Kiara. Lovely to meet you.'

I tried not to look at him even though I could feel him looking at me. He hadn't stopped looking at me since he'd walked into the kitchen. Being on the receiving end of that smoldering, intense gaze made my legs turn from a solid to a liquid. I was about to reach for the fire blanket Rosie kept in the kitchen and throw it over myself.

'It's lovely to meet *you*,' Kiara said earnestly. 'I know you're an engineer. I'm in awe. I'm hopeless at Math and Physics. Nico used to tear his hair out helping me with homework.'

He'd helped her with homework?

I blinked.

I tried to imagine this smooth, sophisticated guy sitting patiently by his sister, helping her with algebra.

'Well that's, er, lovely.' And honestly I *did* think it was lovely. Except that I was confused by the contradictions. 'You came here for your jacket, so I ought to get that for you—'

Nico was still watching me. I wondered if part of his job involved interrogation because his gaze was like a laser. If I'd had a mirror I would have checked there wasn't a red dot on my forehead.

There was a long, pulsing silence and he continued to look at me as if something I'd said had answered a question lingering in his head.

'I'm not here for the jacket. We're here because Rosie invited us to join you for Christmas.'

CHAPTER FIVE

SHE WHAT?

My sister had invited him without telling me.

I didn't know whether to kill her or kiss her.

Kiara was looking anxious. 'It was kind of you to invite us both. Are you sure it's all right?'

No, it wasn't all right.

Why hadn't she told me?

Coward.

I turned my head to look accusingly at Rosie. I felt like yelling 'chicken' but then realised it would confuse people as she currently had her head buried in a turkey.

I produced what I hoped was a smile, but felt closer to the face I pulled when I was on the receiving end of the wax. 'You're welcome.'

'The food is going to be a while,' Rosie said brightly,

'so why don't you just go into the living room and get to know each other better. Chill out and play some games.'

Chill? I was boiling hot. And as for games—there were already enough games going on in this kitchen. Unfortunately no one had told me the rules.

One look at Rosie's face told me she not only thought she'd already played the first game, she was the winner.

She wafted past me and murmured under her breath, 'Happy Christmas. Enjoy your present.'

Nico was my present?

That was what she'd meant when she'd said it would be arriving later?

I wondered if she'd told him he was my gift. I sincerely hoped not, but knowing my sister she probably had.

I followed her into the living room, avoiding his gaze. Not that I was particularly shy or anything, but I'd been thinking about nothing but sex with him for the past four days. I wasn't confident that my eyes wouldn't light up like slot machines.

Thank goodness he couldn't read my mind.

He sat down on the sofa, nudging my laptop to one side. He'd abandoned Tom Ford, presumably because I was now in possession of half of it, and was wearing a pair of black jeans. They molded themselves to his long, powerful legs as if there was nowhere they'd rather be than snuggled against those hard thighs. I didn't blame them. In fact I envied those jeans. Through the gap in the neck of his shirt I could see a hint of dark hair against bronzed flesh.

I was just pondering the etiquette of accepting a gift who didn't know he was your gift, when he reached idly for my laptop.

'I don't normally work on Christmas day, but do you mind if I just check something?'

I opened my mouth to tell him to help himself when I remembered that not only had I not shut my laptop down the night before, but that the last search had been 'vibrator—the Niccolò'.

I flung myself across the room but it was too late. He'd already opened it and I stood, marinating slowly in embarrassment for the second time in less than four days. It seemed I was destined to humiliate myself around this man. First he'd seen the outer me stripped bare, and now he was seeing the inner me similarly naked.

I was doomed.

'Nico can't stop himself checking the court cases.' Kiara walked across the room balancing the bowls of nuts and crisps my sister had given her. 'Normally he does it on his phone, but I unplugged his charger last night, so I'm in trouble.'

Nowhere near as much trouble as I was in.

Shit, shit, *shit*.

I waited for him to skewer me with one of his severe, disapproving looks, but he didn't. Instead he tapped the keyboard with those strong, clever fingers that knew exactly how to drive a woman crazy and checked whatever it was he wanted to check.

His expression didn't flicker. He was the most inscrutable man I'd ever met. In fact he was so calm and controlled, I wondered if maybe my memory was failing me. Maybe I *had* closed that page down. I must have done, or he would have said something or at least given me one of his looks.

The doorbell rang again and other people started streaming into our apartment, leaving me no opportunity to dwell on it.

It was a good job Rosie had bought those extra presents because pretty soon we were up to twelve people. I knew about eight of them, but it didn't really make any difference because I wasn't looking at them anyway. They might as well have not been there for all the impact they made on me. For me there was only one man in the room.

We popped bottles of bubbly, opened presents, then

helped Rosie carry the food to the table. And all the time I was aware of Nico. Kiara had suddenly become the life and soul of the party, but he'd barely opened his mouth. I knew that, because I kept looking at it. I loved the shape of his lips and kept remembering how they'd felt as they'd moved over mine.

'I should give you your jacket.' I blurted the words out, wishing I had a tenth of his control.

'No hurry.'

That was all he was going to say?

The atmosphere was so tense that by the time my sister placed the turkey in the centre of the table I was hotter than any of the food.

Because our table was designed to seat eight at the most, twelve was a squash. I sat down at the end, because at least then I'd be up close and personal with just one other person.

Nico sat down next to me.

My heart bumped. I tried to work out if this was accident or design and decided he wasn't a man who did anything by accident. He didn't look at me and as usual there was nothing in his expression that gave me any clues as to what he was thinking. His arm brushed against mine. We were jammed together like atoms in a molecule. Anyone looking at us would probably have

assumed it was lack of space that necessitated the close-
ness, but I knew differently.

I'd like to say lunch was delicious, but honestly I
couldn't have told you what I ate because Christmas
lunch was all about the man seated next to me.

When he reached across and forked turkey onto my
plate all I saw were lean, bronzed hands and a dusting
of dark hair on his forearms. He'd rolled his sleeves to
the elbow. I guessed that was as close to casual as this
man got.

'Enough?'

I looked at him blankly.

'Turkey,' he said gently and I blinked.

'Yes. Thanks.' What was it about a man's forearms?
Although, if I were honest, it wasn't just his forearms.
It was all of him.

He leaned forward to pick up a dish of potatoes and I
saw the muscle flex in his powerful shoulders. Then he
sat down again and this time he was thigh to thigh with
me. Our legs might as well have been glued together.

I experimented and eased my leg away slightly, but
his followed.

My heart swooped upwards like a paraglider hitting
a thermal, taking my mood with it.

Rosie glanced at me. 'Is it good?'

'Oh, yes.' I focused on my plate even though I knew

she wasn't talking about the turkey. 'Brilliant. *You're brilliant.*'

People were swapping stories about their Christmas traditions, but I didn't hear a word because I had this noisy, happy sound ringing in my head.

Nico was here.

Sitting next to me.

And whatever our relationship had been in the past, right now it was hot and electric.

I decided one of us had to say something or we'd draw attention to ourselves. 'So what sort of lawyer are you?'

He reached for his glass, although I'd noticed earlier that he was drinking water. Maybe he was afraid his control would slip if he drank alcohol. 'A good one.'

'That's not an answer.' I turned my head to look at him and of course that turned out to be a mistake because his wasn't a face you wanted to look away from. I could have stared at him until I'd died of hunger, thirst or frustration, whichever came first. I could tell you at this rate it was going to be frustration.

And of course, he knew. 'You really want to talk about law?'

There ought to be a law preventing a man driving a woman this crazy.

His voice was so soft I knew no one else would be able to hear him.

The blood was pumping through my veins and I could still feel his thigh pressed hard against mine.

I was just about to make a second attempt at polite conversation, when I felt his hand slide over my thigh. The warmth of his palm pressed through my jeans and I almost jumped out of my seat with shock.

I could no longer pretend any of this was an accident or that we were fused together because of a lack of space. He left his hand there, as if testing to see if I was going to jump, jog the table and knock all the glasses over.

When I didn't move, he slid his hand higher up my thigh and no matter what anyone said about some men, I could tell you there was nothing wrong with his sense of direction. He knew *exactly* where he was going.

My stomach clenched. The excitement was almost painful. The chemistry was off the scale. I didn't understand it, and I was good with all the sciences. I could explain nuclear fission but I couldn't explain this. What I felt made no sense at all to me, but that didn't stop me feeling it and also the frustration that came from being in public.

There always seemed to be something between me

and sexual satisfaction. In this case it was denim and a room full of my friends.

I wished I'd worn a dress with stockings instead of skinny jeans and thigh-length boots, but he was obviously a man who didn't let obstacles get in his way because his fingers moved higher and higher until he was pressing right *there*.

I knocked my wine glass over. Fortunately I'd already drunk half of it, so we had a puddle, not a lake.

'Oh, *crap*.'

My sister threw me a look and a napkin. Then she turned back to her neighbour and continued the conversation.

Nico didn't move his hand, nor did he relax the pressure. As I said, obviously not a man to let anything stand in his way. I felt shivery and weak. The atmosphere between us was heavy, thick and so scorching hot I was surprised we hadn't set off the smoke alarm.

I decided I might as well make the most of the thigh-length boots and ran my foot up his calf.

'More turkey, Hayley?' A guy I knew vaguely from Rosie's gym smiled at me from across the table and I smiled back, shook my head and murmured an acceptable response. It was a surprise to me I could still string a sentence together because I was gripped by raw desire and the delicious friction created by Nico's clever, persistent fingers. The frustration was almost unbearable. I decided pleasure this good shouldn't be one-way and slid my hand up his thigh and covered him. If I'd needed confirmation that he felt the same way, I had it now. His erection was a thick, hard ridge under my hand, pressing through the constraining fabric of his jeans. For a moment I was tempted to pull that zip down, but I decided I'd had enough public exposure for one year.

'Answer me a question—' His voice was soft and just for me.

Given where my hand was, I was worried about what the question might be.

'Only the one?' I had millions I wanted to ask him, and then I remembered my resolution to have a sex-only relationship. I'd never done it before, but I was fairly sure a sex-only relationship involved—well, sex only. Asking questions about other things, particularly family, was a fast way of turning it into something I didn't want. 'What's your question?'

At the far end of the table Kiara was laughing with the man from Rosie's gym. Either Nico hadn't noticed, or he didn't care. Obviously he wasn't his sister's keeper.

'Are you broken-hearted?'

He'd asked me the same question at the wedding. I

hadn't answered it. Why would I offer up something so personal to someone who disapproved of me?

But now—?

'No,' I croaked. 'I'm not broken-hearted.'

He turned his head and gave me a look that told me nothing. 'What time does your "friend Christmas" usually end?'

'It's been known to continue until New Year. Once we had a guest who enjoyed himself so much he stayed until we kicked him out on January 1. We were about to start charging him rent.'

His gaze dropped to my mouth and lingered there.

God, he was serious. I mean *really* serious. Most of the time I was pretty silly. My instinct was to joke around a lot, although I'd worked hard to rein that side of me in, especially around Charlie's family, who had made no secret of the fact they found my sense of humour inappropriate (and that was *before* I'd burst out of my dress at the wedding).

Nico confused me. I'd thought he disapproved of me, but here he was with his hand...where it was.

I sensed something lurking behind those layers of ruthless control, something dark layered under the poker face he presented to the world.

I wondered what his secrets were.

Everyone had secrets, didn't they?

I wouldn't have minded discovering a few of his.

For once I wished our apartment were bigger. I loved it, but it wasn't big enough for me to vanish to the bedroom without all twelve people around the table noticing. It was a miracle they hadn't already noticed what was going on under the turkey. It was a good job Christmas was chaotic.

I really should have helped clear the table, but honestly I couldn't stand up, let alone walk. All that gentle under-table stroking had driven me crazy. I was so, *so* close and the building desperation was killing me and yet still he was relentless, stroking and teasing until I had to clamp my thighs together to stop him.

I could feel him throbbing under my hand. Turning my head to look at him I met his gaze and saw that his eyes were darker than usual. Almost black. I shivered, wondering what it would take to make him drop his guard the way he had at the wedding. I'd never seen him laugh, but it occurred to me I'd never seen him show any other emotion either. Except desire. There was no missing that. It simmered in the depths of those black eyes and pulsed between both of us. I looked at his mouth and remembered how it had felt when we'd kissed. I knew that jaw would feel rough against my palms, because I'd had my hands on it only days earlier. I wanted to have my hands on it again.

I was so absorbed by him I was only dimly aware of my sister bringing in the Christmas pudding, a perfect dome of alcohol-infused dried fruit brought as a gift by one of our guests. Rosie had put holly in the centre, doused it in more alcohol and set fire to it in traditional British style. What wasn't so traditional was that as she put it down on the table, the flame licked one of the napkins. It caught fire.

Nico was on his feet instantly. Calmly, he doused the flames with a jug of water and then grabbed a pile of napkins and mopped up the water before it could do more damage. And all without ruining the pudding.

'Hey, quick work.' My sister looked shaken but she smiled at Nico and then at me, as if she was approving my choice.

I was starting to approve of my choice, too. The man might be a little uncommunicative, but he was good to have around in a crisis. First my dress, and now this. He wasn't a man who hesitated. And I liked the way he helped my sister with clearing the table before sitting down again.

I was surprised our little fire hadn't set off the smoke alarm, but Nico and I were producing far more heat than the flames on that pudding, so the smoke alarm was probably unconscious by now.

I'd stopped eating and so had he. I wished there was

a way to make Christmas lunch go on forever because I didn't want today to end. But of course in real life good things always ended.

'We have to leave now.' He spoke softly so that no one else could hear, not that they were paying any attention to us anyway. They were too wrapped up in Christmas pudding and conversation.

'Of course.' I hadn't expected him to leave quite this soon and the level of disappointment appalled me. The whole idea of a sex-based relationship was to avoid these emotional lows. Clearly I was doing something wrong. 'I'm sure you and Kiara have lots to do.'

'I'm not leaving with Kiara,' he said calmly. 'I'm leaving with you.'

'Me?' My mouth was drier than overcooked turkey breast. The same couldn't be said for the part of me that was under his fingers. 'I can't leave. I live here. It's Christmas.'

He glanced at our friends, most of whom were by now laughing uncontrollably. 'They're happy. And I need to give you my gift.'

'You bought me a gift? You didn't have to do that.' I felt a little embarrassed because obviously I didn't have anything for him. Presumably he'd considered it an obligation to his host. 'Why didn't you just give it to Rosie when you arrived?'

'It isn't for Rosie. It's for you. It's personal.'

'You could give it to me here.'

'I don't think so.' He reached for his glass and I noticed that he was still drinking water. I wondered again whether this was all part of his determination to hang onto control. It scared me how badly I wanted to push him and rip it all back until I exposed the real him, but maybe that was because I'd been nothing but exposed in the past week, so it was definitely his turn.

'Why not?'

'Because my gift is just for you. Not to be shared.'

'How do you know it's something I want?' I jumped as someone popped a cork on another bottle of champagne. The movement increased the friction against his hand and I almost moaned.

'I know it's something you want, Hayley.'

'How?'

'Because you'd already typed it into a search engine on your laptop.'

I was so distracted by the sensations exploding through my body, it took a moment for his words to sink in.

When they did, I turned my head again.

His eyes were velvet dark and locked on mine. There was a faint gleam of humour there, and something else—something that made my stomach twist and spin and then drop like a stone from a high cliff.

'My laptop?'

He leaned closer. His lips brushed my ear. 'Did you manage to locate 'The Niccolò'?'

Heat poured over me and warmth pooled in my pelvis. If he was waiting for me to respond, he was going to be waiting a long time. I couldn't form a word let alone a sentence. I made an inarticulate sound that drew Rosie's attention.

She frowned slightly, satisfied herself I didn't need the Heimlich manoeuvre and drew everyone's attention to herself by telling a funny joke that required sound effects and hand gestures.

Did I mention I loved my sister?

Nico didn't seem to care what anybody else at the table thought. He was focused just on me and it was the sexiest, most intense experience of my life. Charlie had looked over my shoulder most of the time, as if conversing with me was an irritation he had to endure. The boyfriend I'd had before him used to just start talking about himself.

I'd never had a man look at me the way this man was looking at me.

As if everyone else in the room was inconsequential.

'I don't know what you're talking about.'

His eyes were two shimmering pools of dark promise. 'No? Because I happen to know where you can find
what you were looking for.'

God, his voice was sexy. And the way his breath
warmed my neck. I quivered and shivered. 'You do?'

'Yes.' I could hear the smile in his voice and feel the
sure, confident slide of his hand between my shaking
thighs. 'But you'll have to come with me.'

'You're suggesting I leave my own Christmas party?'

'You haven't talked to anyone else since we sat down.'

A burst of raucous laughter brought me back to the
present and I glanced at Rosie, who winked at me and
raised her glass.

A different person might have scowled at the thought
of being left with the washing up, but Rosie wasn't
like that.

She'd set this up for me.

This was my Christmas present.

I owed it to her to make the most of it.

Deciding that this was one gift I was going to un-
wrap in private, I pushed my plate away and turned to
Nico. 'Let's go.'

CHAPTER SIX

HIS CAR WAS still the same low red Ferrari. A growling gas-guzzling trophy of Italian engineering perfection.

I wondered if I was supposed to play it cool and pretend I travelled in cars like this all the time. Then I remembered he'd seen me half-exposed in a torn dress and found my computer search. Cool had flown the nest. I sank into expensive leather and sighed.

'Do you realise this has a 4.5 litre V8 engine? They reduced the piston compression height as they do in a racing engine. Oh, God, I love it. I want to crawl all over it and lick it.' I restricted myself to stroking the dashboard. 'I suppose being Italian, you have to have a car like this. You're not compensating for deficiencies in your masculinity, are you?

His response was a slow smile because of course I already knew the answer to that question. I'd eaten Christmas lunch with one hand on his masculinity.

It was the first time I'd seen him smile and it was worth waiting for. It pulled his mouth into a sexy curve that hinted at more hidden layers. I stared for a moment, fascinated. There was so much more to this man and I couldn't wait to uncover those parts—all of them.

This promised to be the best Christmas day I'd had in a long time.

Glancing in the mirror, he pulled smoothly away from the curb and down the empty streets.

It was still snowing. The Ferrari should have been a nightmare to drive in these conditions, but he didn't seem to have any problems.

Nico Rossi was a man who seemed to take everything in his stride, be it split dresses, table fires or a lethal road surface.

'So I guess the ability to drive fast cars is in Italian DNA.'

Risking life and limb, I put my hand between his thighs.

'*Cristo*—' He breathed in sharply but kept his eyes on the road and his hands on the wheel. Impressive. As I said, this man had iron control. 'You didn't know

Kiara and I were coming today. I assumed Rosie had discussed it with you.'

'No. She sprung it on me.'

Cursing softly, he pulled in to the side of the road, the movement so sudden I was surprised the airbag didn't smack me in the face. 'Tell me the truth.' He spoke through his teeth and his eyes were a dark flash of molten passion.

I couldn't believe I'd ever thought him cold. 'About what?'

'About how you feel. I need you to be honest.'

I had no problem with honesty. I preferred it, even though honesty meant exposing yourself. Not the split dress type of exposing—the other type. 'I'm in your car. That should tell you how I feel.'

'I just want us both to be clear about what this is.'

I'd forgotten he was a lawyer. 'You want me to sign a contract or something?'

He shot me an exasperated look and I shrugged.

'Sorry, just checking. If you expect me to read your mind, you'll have to give me more clues. You don't reveal anything about yourself. Most of the time I can't even tell whether you're happy or sad.'

'What about turned on?' His voice vibrated, low and sexy. 'Can you tell when I'm turned on?'

I thought about how he felt under my hand. 'Those clues are easier to read.'

'They're the only clues you need.' His gaze held mine. 'I want you.'

It shouldn't have turned me on to hear that, but it did. In fact it was exactly what I wanted to hear. I didn't want anything else.

I wondered if the Ferrari came with a sprinkler system because I was fairly sure I was going to burst into flames at any moment.

'Fine by me. My New Year's resolution is to just have sex without the complicated, totally-messed-up relationship part.'

His eyes narrowed, as if he didn't believe me and his scepticism didn't surprise me. Why would it? We could put a man on the moon, but apparently we couldn't convince the majority of the male population that a woman could want sex without needing to hear the *L* word. I didn't have any reason to believe Nico Rossi was different to the average man.

There was a long, tense silence. Snow drifted onto the windscreen.

'Tell me how you felt at the wedding.'

'Honestly? I can't really explain it. Obviously you're an incredibly good kisser. And you're good at other things, too. I was excited. Turned on. Exasperated that both our sisters chose to knock when they did—' I stopped, thinking I'd pretty much summed it all up.

There was a long, pulsing pause and then he breathed deeply.

'I was asking how you felt about seeing Charlie marry another woman.'

'Oh...'

So now instead of a sprinkler system I had humiliation, washing over my skin like boiling oil, seeping into my pores and heating me up until I thought I might vaporise.

I'd been telling him how strongly I felt about him and all the time he'd been asking about Charlie.

I'd revealed so much. *Too much.*

Which was the story of my life if you thought about it.

Metaphorically and literally, my whole life was a ripped dress.

'Right. Well, this is embarrassing.'

'No, it isn't.'

'Not for you, maybe, but you're not the one who just put herself out there.'

'You weren't broken-hearted?'

'If we're going for honesty here, then I'd like to know why you kissed me when you don't even like me.

I'm all for sex with no complications, but self-esteem demands it's at least with someone who likes who I am.'

His gaze was steady. 'Did you really think I would have had my hand up your dress if I didn't like you?'

'You're a man. Men do that sort of thing all the time.'

He flipped on the wipers, cleared the snow from his windscreen and pulled back into the road. 'Some men make decisions based on something more than a surge of testosterone.'

He shifted gears smoothly and the engine purred, loving his skilled touch. I sympathised.

I shifted in my seat so that I could look at his face. It was past six o'clock and anywhere else in the country it would have been dark, but in London it was as if someone had forgotten to turn the lights off. The place blazed like the runway at Heathrow airport. 'Are you angry?'

It was a moment before he answered. 'Thinking about you with Charlie makes me angry. Why the hell were you with him, Hayley? He constantly tried to make you someone you weren't.'

'That isn't true.'

'When you got this job, did he help you celebrate? No, he got drunk.'

And Nico had driven me home.

As my sister had reminded me, it had been Nico who had dropped me safely at my door.

My heart hammered against my chest. It felt like a wake-up call because he was asking me the question I should have asked myself right from day one. 'I know you disapprove of me.'

As usual his expression revealed nothing. 'You don't know anything, Hayley.'

He pulled up at a junction.

The lights were on red and I found myself looking at the flex of thigh muscle as he stopped the car. And then he turned his head and I glanced from his leg to his face. I felt like a teenager unable to stop staring at the best looking boy in the class. Right at that moment no one else existed for me. We could have been the only two people on an alien planet where lights blazed and the streets were empty.

'I don't want to talk about Charlie.' His voice had a rough quality that rubbed over my nerve endings and made me shiver.

'OK.' It wasn't exactly an eloquent response, but it was the best I could manage with him looking at me like that.

'And just for the record, I can't explain what happened at the wedding either.' There was an edge to his voice. 'It wasn't like me.'

One look at Kiara's face had told me that.

Now I couldn't speak at all. My insides were quivery. Warmth spread through me because right now I was the woman he was with and I didn't care what had happened before or what might come after.

The lights had changed, but he didn't move and neither did I.

We were locked together by a shocking chemistry and a total inability to look away.

Honestly, whenever this sort of thing happened in the movies I rolled my eyes. Although admittedly in the movies the heroine was staring at someone like Ryan Gosling, which maybe made the whole 'struck by lightning' thing slightly more believable.

But I hadn't ever imagined it could happen in real life to an everyday person like me.

The connection was so intense and powerful I wanted to bottle it. I wanted to feel that same revved-up level of excitement for the rest of my life. Or maybe I didn't. I wouldn't be able to eat or sleep feeling like this.

I thought about *Groundhog Day* and decided if I could stay in a moment forever it would be this one, suspended in the blissful, almost unbearable excitement of what was to come without any of the trauma afterwards.

Maybe with my New Year's resolution, all my relationships would feel like this. I'd live the excitement,
then walk away before the collapse part.

A horn sounded behind us and I realised we weren't
the only people on the roads.

Nico swore softly and turned his attention back to
the car.

He was driving towards the river and I realised I
hadn't even asked where he lived. I didn't know where
he was taking me.

We drove along the embankment, past the Albert
Bridge. It was my favorite bridge in London. Elegant
and floodlit, it sent sparkles of light over the inky black
surface of the water below. When I was little it used to
make me think of a woman putting on diamonds for
an exciting night out. Rosie called it the Bling Bridge.
I didn't believe in fairy tales, but if I did, this bridge
would definitely have featured in mine.

We were in Chelsea and I expected him to drive
south because I didn't know anyone who could afford
to live here, but he suddenly swooped into an underground car park.

It was spacious and well lit, but away from the bright
lights of the city, the truth suddenly hit me. I was with
a man I barely knew.

The blood pulsed in my ears and then he reached

across and undid my seat belt. 'It's cold. We should
go up.'

Cold? I wasn't cold. I was burning hot.

I was also having second thoughts, despite reminding myself that the fact we barely knew each other
was supposed to be a good thing. That was the *point*
of emotionless sex.

And it wasn't as if he was a stranger. We'd bumped
into each other on and off for years, just never really
spoken. But honestly, how well did any of us ever really know anyone? My mum was married to my dad
for fifteen years before she found out he was having
affairs. She'd trusted him. I'd been with Charlie for
ten months and he'd behaved in ways that made it obvious to me I'd never known him. All we knew about
another person was what they chose to show us. You
could only know someone if they let you know them.

His apartment was on the top floor and my jaw was
also on the floor because it was the penthouse, com-
plete with balcony and views over the river towards
my fairy-tale bridge.

'Wow.' As praise went, it wasn't that eloquent, but it
was all I could manage. Honestly, I was dumbstruck.
How the hell could he afford this? 'What sort of lawyer did you say you were again?' He'd told me he was a
good one. It was obvious he was a very, *very* good one.

'Do you really want to talk about work?'

His voice came from right behind me and I turned and saw that he was holding a bottle of champagne.

I was surprised. 'You didn't drink anything at lunchtime.'

'I knew I'd be driving you home.'

I licked my lips. 'What if I'd said no?5'

'I was in possession of evidence that suggested you wouldn't.' His response was sure and confident. The corners of his mouth flickered and he eased the cork out of the champagne like a pro. By now I was so jumpy and on edge that when it popped, I flinched.

'I don't see how a few words typed into a search engine could be used as evidence. Several people had access to that laptop, including yourself.'

He raised an eyebrow and poured me the sparkling liquid into a tall, thin-stemmed glass.

I didn't want to be impressed, but I was.

Rosie and I only drank champagne if someone else bought it and we never drank out of glasses like these. It made it feel special. He made *me* feel special. I wondered what he'd thought of our apartment with its non-matching plates and table designed to seat half the number of people we'd squashed around it.

His home was all polished wood and soft leather.

'What are we celebrating?' I watched as the bubbles

rose and wondered what it was about champagne that lifted the mood. 'Christmas?'

'You. Naked in my apartment.'

My tummy tightened. 'I'm still dressed.'

His eyes met mine and he handed me a glass. 'Not for long.'

My pulse was racing and I lifted my glass. 'Merry Christmas.'

'Buon Natale! Salute!'

Oh, God, Italian was a hot language.

We drank and the champagne fizzed in my mouth and spread through my veins. Or maybe it was the chemistry that was fizzing, but whatever it was I could feel it all the way through me. 'The only Italian I know is *Pizza Margherita*. And you're the first Italian man I've met.'

The corners of his mouth flickered. 'I'm Sicilian.'

'Like Al Pacino.'

'Al Pacino was born in New York.'

Shut up, Hayley. 'I'll stop talking.'

'Don't,' he breathed and he turned to put his champagne glass down on the low glass table. '*Don't* stop talking. I like it.'

'You like it when I talk crap?'

'You're not talking crap. You're just nervous.' He removed my glass from my hand and I should have objected, not just because I was enjoying the champagne but because after Charlie I didn't want any man telling me when I could or couldn't drink.

'Actually—'

'I like it when you don't censor what you say and do.'

Just when I was ready to punch him, he said something like that.

'You didn't look as if you liked it when my dress gave way.'

'I didn't want all those wedding guests having heart attacks. I didn't think the hospital could cope with a major incident that close to Christmas.'

I was laughing and blushing at the same time because it was impossible to remember it without also remembering the moments we'd shared. 'I still don't know what happened.'

'The inevitable happened.'

'Not true. I'm not saying it hadn't crossed my mind but not in a million years did I really think it would happen.'

He paused. 'I wasn't talking about the dress.'

'Neither was I.' I was eye level with his throat and I could see the dark stubble shadowing his jaw. I'd seen the Grand Canyon and Niagara Falls, but I decided there weren't many better views than this one. 'I just didn't ever see us together. I didn't think you liked who I was.'

'I didn't like who you were when you were with Charlie, because that wasn't the real you. You were constantly trying to rein yourself in.' He stroked his finger over my jaw, studying me and I gulped, wondering how he knew so much.

'Maybe you're not going to like the real me.'

'Hayley, I saw who you were the first time I met you. I spotted you across the room and you were so full of energy, so excited about your topic that I moved closer because I had to hear what you were saying.'

'Probably something boring.' The truth was I'd noticed him, too. 'It was at Charlie's party. Two years ago.'

'Twenty months, two weeks, two days.'

I choked on the champagne. 'Is that a lawyer thing? Remembering the tiny details?'

He looked at me steadily. 'Some things stay in my head.'

'You didn't talk to me that night.'

He gave a funny smile. 'You were talking to Charlie. And after that, I never saw that same excitement again. You reined it in.'

'Charlie didn't get too excited about satellites. Except the sort that gave him the sports channel.'

'He molded you into a different person and you were so anxious to keep the relationship going, you went along with it.'

Ashamed though I was to admit it, it was all true. I suppose I'd needed to know I could hold on to a man if I'd wanted to. Turned out I couldn't.

Little by little, I'd subdued my real self. I'd stopped talking about my work when we went out and smiled when Charlie had talked about his. It had happened a bit at a time, so I barely noticed I was doing it. I was like the Arctic fox who changed his coat from brown to white in the winter to blend into his surroundings. On the inside I was the same, but on the outside I blended with the crowd. I'd never been in a relationship that worked on any other level. Never been with anyone, apart from my sister, who only ever expected me to be *me*.

But I had no idea how Nico knew that.

'I thought you disapproved of me being with him.'

He lowered his head and leaned his forehead against mine. 'I did. It was like giving a Ferrari to someone who only ever drives to the supermarket. A tragic waste.'

'No man has ever compared me to a Ferrari before.' To me, it was a compliment. And so was the way he was looking at me, as if I was the best Christmas present any guy could be given.

'He was wrong for you in every way.'

I wasn't going to argue with that. Especially not right now when Nico was moments away from kissing me. I wished I had a tenth of his control. Given that I'd been waiting all day for this moment I thought I was showing great restraint. I discovered I actually quite liked the slow, desperate build of anticipation and maybe he did, too, because instead of bringing his mouth down on mine, he gave a half smile and slid his fingers through my hair. It didn't matter what he did with his fingers, which part of me he was stroking— it always had the same effect on me. I'd thought about nothing but being kissed by him for the past three days and the wait was killing me. It didn't help that we'd driven each other mad all day.

I broke first.

One moment I had my hand locked in the front of his shirt. The next I was undoing buttons. Finally. The big reveal. 'You saw me naked from the waist up. You owe me.'

His mouth hovered close to mine, but still he didn't kiss me. He was either a skilled torturer or he knew everything there was to know about delayed gratification.

'I always pay my debts.' His eyes were half shut and the way he was looking at me made my stomach flip.

I had his shirt undone to the waist and my fingers went all fumbly, mostly because I saw sex in his eyes. I lost patience and yanked the shirt. Buttons skittered and bounced over the pale wooden floor, but I was too busy looking at the smooth, powerful contours of his chest through the shadowing of dark hair.

Oh, Santa, Santa, what have you brought me this year…

His eyes darkened. 'You just ripped my shirt.'

'Sorry.' Never in the history of apologies had an apology sounded less sincere. I wasn't sorry at all, and just to prove it I slid my hands slowly up his chest. I felt hard muscle and the steady beat of his heart. 'You saw me in a ripped dress, so now we're even.'

'You seem to have a thing about ripping clothes.' The gleam in his eyes made it hard to breathe.

'It's Christmas. You're allowed to rip open your Christmas presents. And anyway, I figured if you can afford to live here, you can afford another shirt.' I pushed the shirt off those muscular shoulders and sucked in a breath because there, curling over the top of his biceps, was a symbol inked into his flesh.

I think my heart might have stopped. It definitely did something strange in my chest.

'OK, well, that's—' I breathed and stared at it for a

moment. Then I lifted my hand and traced it with the tips of my fingers. 'Surprising.' Not in a million years would I have expected this man to have a tattoo. 'I thought you were this ruthlessly controlled, conservative, Eton-then-straight-to-Oxford type.'

'Did you?' His husky question slid against my knees and weakened them.

I thought about the wedding, when I'd spent a good ten minutes staring at him acknowledging the raw, elemental quality that lurked beneath the beautifully cut suit. About that car journey, when the tension had almost fried both of us. I'd always known what lay beneath the surface.

'I guess I made assumptions.'

'People do that. They look and they think they know. And sometimes they don't look because they don't want to know.'

'Charlie—'

'I don't want to talk about Charlie any more.'

Neither did I.

I wondered how a man who never showed emotion could be so perceptive. So in tune with my feelings. It unsettled me. I was used to people believing in the person I presented to the world. I chose how much of myself I revealed. Discounting the day of the wedding where I'd revealed far more than I'd wanted to, I didn't show much.

I thought about all the parts of myself I'd never shared with anyone. Thoughts that were all mine and not for sharing.

'Tell me about the tattoo.'

'A tattoo is just on the surface. You and I are going deeper than that.'

I swallowed. *We were?*

'A tattoo isn't who I am any more than a ripped dress is who you are.' His mouth was closer to mine. I could feel the warmth of his breath against my lips.

I'd got used to thinking relationships were mostly fake and superficial, but this didn't feel either of those things. There was nothing fake about the way his tongue traced the seam of my lips. Nothing fake about the way his hands eased my hips into his, and certainly nothing fake about the thickness of the erection I felt throbbing against me.

I leaned forward and pressed my mouth to his shoulder. The tattoo shocked me because it was so unexpected. I'd always known there was so much more to him. I ran my fingers down the swell of hard muscle, feeling the leashed power under the dark ink of his tattoo. I heard the slight change in his breathing and could feel him fighting for control.

'You hold yourself back.' I thought about how ruthlessly he held himself in check and wondered what had made him like that. 'Who are you really?'

'Does it matter?' He cupped my face in his hands and his voice had a raw edge to it that was impossibly exciting.

I remembered my resolution to have uncomplicated sex with a hot man. They didn't come any hotter than Nico.

'No.' I silenced the questions in my head, telling myself they weren't relevant to the moment. 'I want you.'

The corner of his mouth tilted into the sexiest smile I'd ever seen. He might not smile often, but when he did he did it *really* well. His mouth hovered wickedly close to mine until I was afraid I might knock him over and damage him in my haste and desperation to finish what we'd started at the wedding.

And then finally, after days of my waiting and thinking of nothing else, he lowered his head and kissed me.

CHAPTER SEVEN

AS I'D BEEN thinking of nothing else for days I thought my mind had probably exaggerated his skill at kissing. It should have been a disappointment. It wasn't. It was as good as I remembered. Better, because this time he was half-naked, too, and I finally had full access to his ripped body. His hand was hard on my back and I could feel the warmth of his palm pressing through my shirt, flattening me against him. God, he was strong. He had the body of a fighter. I knew. I'd seen plenty when I'd been to Rosie's gym and I knew this man could have kept pace with all of them.

After the almost intolerable build-up of the past few days I was desperate, but he kept it slow, torturing both of us with pleasure.

I moaned as his mouth slid to my neck. 'I hate to

rush something so good, but I think I might need you to—' The words died as my shirt slid to the floor. I hadn't even felt him undo the buttons and he must have done it with one hand. I remembered what else he could do with his fingers and shivered in anticipation. He was smooth, skilled and in control whereas I just wanted to crawl all over him like a desperate puppy and lick his face. OK, not just his face. All of him.

I slid my hands down his chest (oh, my *God*), lingered over his hard abs and then moved to the snap of his jeans just as his hands parted my shirt.

His eyes darkened, but there was a glimmer of amusement. 'You're wearing a bra.'

'Of course.' I stared up at him, deadpan. 'I would never be seen in public without a bra, Your Honour.'

He traced the line of fur with one finger. 'I'm not a judge.'

'Everyone's a judge, especially where I'm concerned.'

'In that case, I'm going to declare you guilty.' His voice was husky and I found myself looking at his mouth. That wicked, sinful line of sensual torture. I didn't care that he rarely used it to smile. I wanted him to use it for other things and I wanted him to do it right now. I was at the point of explosion.

'If I'm guilty, then I'll take whatever punishment I

have coming, but just get on with it. I'm ready to pay the price for my sins.'

'I like your festive bra, but it's going to have to come off.'

I didn't even feel his hand move but the silky bra slithered to the floor after my shirt. For the second time in a week Nico had an uninterrupted view of my bare breasts. Just for a moment I felt shy, which was ridiculous when you thought about how we'd got to this point.

Maybe it was because up until now it hadn't mattered what he thought of me.

I was totally hopeless at this unemotional sex thing.

I tried to focus on the physical.

'*Cristo*, you have the most incredible breasts.' His voice was raw and the look in his eyes removed shyness.

'There are plenty of people who wouldn't agree with you. Like most of the guests at the wedding.'

'They all agreed with me, *dolcezza*. That was the problem.' His mouth was on mine and he powered me back to the sofa. I fell backwards, off balance in every single way, but he caught me and lowered me carefully, like those couples you see doing a very sexy tango. God, he was strong. Then he came down on top of me like a conquering hero, his hand on my thigh.

'I love your thigh-length boots,' he breathed, 'but

they're going to have to come off, too. I want you naked. In fact I want *you*. Now.'

His words turned me on almost as much as the look in his eyes. All I could think of was him.

Us.

Together.

His hands were on my boots and I was about to give him instructions because they were really awkward to remove, when he slid them off my legs. When *I* did it there was loads of tugging and swearing and falling over and yelling for Rosie. He managed to do it in one perfect movement. Same with my jeans. Not a man to let anything stand in his way.

I swallowed. 'So you're obviously good at undressing women—'

'Let's just say in this case I'm motivated.'

I was naked apart from the red thong trimmed with white fur and I decided it needed some explanation.

'Rosie gave it to me for Christmas.'

'You look like Santa's sexy little helper.' He slid a lazy finger over the fur. 'It looks much too hot to be worn indoors.'

It suddenly occurred to me that I was all but naked and he was still clothed.

'It's your turn. Strip.'

One eyebrow lifted. 'Are you giving me orders?'

'You give people orders all the time.'

Eyes mocking, he rose to his feet and stood there for a moment just watching me, legs spread, powerful chest on display and his hands on his zip.

'What do you want me to do, Hayley? Tell me.'

His use of my name made the whole thing more intimate. No matter how much I kidded myself, we weren't strangers. Far from it. We'd circled round each other for years.

As he slid his zip down, my eyes saw what my hand already knew and my mouth dried. The same couldn't be said for other parts of me. I was desperate. I squirmed on his sofa. 'Hurry up. This is an emergency.'

He undressed swiftly and gracefully, but that didn't surprise me. Everything about him was controlled.

Actually, not everything.

There was one part of him he couldn't control and that part was thrusting hard against a pair of black boxer briefs. I felt sympathy for those briefs. Containing an erection of that size just wasn't in the job description. If I'd needed evidence he felt the same way I did, I had it now.

My gaze fixed on the line of dark hair that disappeared beneath the waistband. I needed to see where it ended. 'You're going to be hot in those.'

He slid them off and I stopped joking. Honestly,

there was nothing to joke about. The atmosphere had snapped tight. I knew he felt it, too.

A muscle worked in his lean jaw and I could almost feel the battle he was fighting. Tension throbbed from those sleek, powerful muscles. With a soft curse he came back down on top of me, removing the last barrier between us so I was as naked as him. '*Cristo*, I promised myself I was going to make this last—'

'We've made it last for days.' I slid my palms down his back, savouring the feel of sleek skin over hard muscle. He was heavy, but I loved the way it felt having him like this. 'Longest foreplay ever.' The roughness of his thigh grazed the softness of mine as he pushed my thighs apart.

Our eyes were locked together. I could have looked at him all day. He was the most spectacular man I'd ever seen and if I was honest, part of me couldn't quite believe I was doing this. With him. Not that I undersold myself or anything, but men like him didn't come along very often. I knew, because I'd been looking for long enough. I wanted to grab my iPhone and take a picture, just so I could prove it to myself later. I wanted to post his picture on Twitter (would have got me at least 40,000 new followers, I can tell you) to increase my street cred, but then I felt his hand move lower and he stroked that quivering, damp part of me with sure, skillful fingers and I stopped thinking about anything except the moment, and he was a man who knew exactly how to make the most of the moment.

I think I moaned, and that was probably uncool but there was no way to keep the sound inside while he was touching me the way he was touching me. His fingers were knowing and clever, sliding over me and into me in exactly the right way and I knew from the way he was looking at me, at the way he kissed me, that this was just the beginning of what we were going to do together. I was about to tell him I couldn't stand it any longer when he eased away from me and worked his way down my body. He started at my neck and then moved lower and by the time he'd teased and toyed with my nipples I was squirming with desperation. It was almost too much to bear.

When he moved lower, I shifted restlessly but he clamped his hands on my hips and pushed my legs apart, giving himself full access. The first stroke of his tongue made me gasp and I soon discovered he was as talented with that part of himself as he was with his fingers. Each skilled flick of his tongue, each slow, delicious stroke was designed to drive me crazy and it did. I tried to move my hips, tried desperately to relieve the almost intolerable ache, but the hard grip of his hands were holding me still. Not that he was hurting me, but it was obvious there was no way I was moving until he was ready to let me go. I was totally at his mercy and I'd never known excitement this intense. I needed to come, but he wouldn't let me. Deprived of any other outlet, I dug my fingers into the soft cushions of his sofa.

'Please, *please*—' I couldn't believe I was begging. I'd never begged a man for anything in my life and I knew I was going to be horribly embarrassed later, but I seemed to spend my whole life in a state of embarrassment around this guy, so I figured at this point it wasn't going to make much difference. 'Nico, I really need—' My words were disjointed, mostly because his tongue was inside me, licking me shamelessly, and now he was using his fingers, too, so that my body was a mass of delicious, shivering sensation hovering on the edge of the incredible. And I was on the edge. Right on the edge. If he hadn't been holding me firmly I could have moved my hips and finished it myself. But instead of letting me do that, he eased away from me slightly, leaving me hovering between ecstasy and insanity.

'Tell me what you need, *dolcezza*.'

As if I wasn't already desperate enough, now he had to speak to me in Italian, the bastard. His Italian accent and the way he lingered over the word *dolcezza* almost finished me off.

'You know what I need—' I couldn't believe he could be so cruel, but then he put his mouth on me again and I forgave him everything. Every provocative slide of his tongue was designed to torment me—only, this time he gave me what I wanted.

It was the most intense experience of my life. Everything inside me tightened and then orgasm crashed down on me, the rush of pleasure almost agonizing. And still he held my hips, controlling everything I was feeling until I lay limp and weak.

I thought I heard him murmur, 'Merry Christmas, Hayley', but I could have imagined it.

Then he reached down and pulled something from the pocket of his jeans. I'd thought I'd never want to see a condom again after the wedding, but it turned out I was wrong.

I lay dazed, watching as he sheathed himself and then came down over me. I was worried I'd be too sensitive, but just looking at him made me want him again and I wrapped my legs around him and felt his hand slide underneath my buttocks, lifting me. My breathing was shallow and my cheeks were burning, but I didn't think the heat had anything to do with the flames flickering in the fireplace. It was him.

I was glad our first time was going to be this way because I wanted to look at him.

And he obviously wanted to look at me, too, because he kissed me again, holding my gaze as he shifted his position. I felt him against me, felt him hard and smooth against the slippery wetness he'd created and I held my breath. Still, he took his time. His mouth seduced mine, his hand was hard on my bottom and his gaze was locked with mine and finally he was inside me, sliding deep in a series of slow, expert thrusts. Oh, *God*. It felt incredible. I didn't think I could feel like this again so soon. He was hard and thick and I could feel him pulse inside me, feel his own battle to hold back the primal, primitive desire that had sunk its teeth into both of us. He stopped for a moment, his breathing unsteady and I sort of understood because I wanted it to last, too, but I was also desperate. I dug my fingers into the smooth, solid bulk of his shoulders and rocked into him. I felt the tension and strain in his muscles increase.

'*Cristo*, Hayley—' His eyes were impossibly dark and then he gave a groan and surged into me, and I knew he was as out of control as I was. He was deep inside me, moving with a perfect rhythm and I cried out because I'd never felt anything like it. Never. Until a few days before we'd never touched each other, and yet somehow he knew my body. He knew just how to move, how to touch me, how to adjust the angle and the rhythm of his movements so that I felt every inch of him. With each expert thrust he drove me higher and higher and all the time I could feel him, all of him, strength, power, masculinity and I moved with him, my hands on his shoulders and then buried in his hair.

He'd dimmed the lights, but the room was lit by the dancing flames of the fire and the glow of the city at night. We were surrounded by glass and the London skyline. It was like having sex outdoors, only without the risk of frostbite. Afterwards I realised that anyone with a pair of binoculars might have been able to see us from the apartments on the other side of the river, but I didn't even think about it at the time and neither did he. We were just too into each other.

The whole of me was trembling and held in a state of heightened suspension. I shouldn't have been this desperate, but I was, and so was he. He said something to me in Italian, his lips dragging along my jaw and then lingering on my mouth. Presumably he didn't expect me to answer him, which was a good thing because I wasn't capable of speech. I didn't know whether it was all the foreplay under the Christmas lunch table, whether this whole thing had been building since the wedding or whether this was sex Italian style (if so, I was emigrating), but I couldn't hold anything back. Feelings and sensations spread through me. It started somewhere I couldn't identify, deep in my soul, and then filtered and rippled through my body until I came in a glorious rush of pulsing pleasure. I felt myself tighten around him and heard him groan in his throat as he tried to hold on to control, but the ripples of my orgasm sent him over the edge.

I heard him curse, but he was lost just as I was, and in a way I was relieved his grip on control was as useless as mine. If he could have detached himself from pleasure this intense I would have been worried.

We didn't stop kissing. Not once. Not as he thrust hard, or as my body gripped his—we just kept kissing and his tongue was in my mouth and mine in his and we just shared all of it. Everything. Every pulse, throb, flutter, moan and gasp.

One of my hands was jammed into his hair, the other clutching his shoulder, now slick with sweat, and I lay for a moment stunned and shaken, just staring up at him trying to make sense of it.

I didn't know what was going to happen next. After all, this level of intimacy was new to both of us. I suppose part of me, the part responsible for self-protection, was braced for him to just roll away. And I suppose if he'd done that I would have said something like, 'Well, I think "The Niccolò" is a product with a future,' or something really glib that wouldn't reveal how deeply the whole experience had affected me.

I thought that was probably what someone would say after emotionless sex.

But he didn't roll away. He didn't pull away. Instead he slowly, gently lowered his mouth to mine and kissed me again. But it was different now. This was a different type of intimacy. It was slow, sexy with a hint of gentleness that made my heart squeeze. I hadn't expected tenderness. Even as I felt myself melt, I felt a faint flicker of panic. My heart was the one organ that wasn't invited to this party.

This was where he was supposed to do that classic man thing and say and do the wrong thing so that I could flounce back to Notting Hill and spend the rest of the night curled up with Rosie agreeing that men weren't just from Mars—most of them were from a galaxy far, far away. But he didn't. He lingered over the kiss, pushed my hair gently back from my face and studied me for a moment and then rolled onto his side and pulled me against him. If he'd done that in my apartment we would have both ended up on the floor, but fortunately his sofa was bigger than ours. His arms held me in a possessive grip and it surprised me. I'd thought him cold and distant and had wrongly taken that to mean he wasn't good at intimacy. On the other hand I hadn't anticipated the tattoo either, which just proved I was clueless about this man.

Because I had no choice in the matter I stayed where I was, locked in the circle of his arms, my head on his chest. The differences between us fascinated me and I lay there, absorbing the contrast. My blonde hair draped itself all over him and mingled with the dark hairs on his chest. My skin looked creamy pale against the warmer tones of his. The inner skin of my thigh was soft against the hardness of his.

He lifted his hand and twisted a strand of my hair around his fingers and I wondered if he was noticing the differences, too.

I'd never been the sort to lean on a man, probably because when I was growing up I'd learned first-hand that leaning was a lethal sport that inevitably ended in serious injury. My mum had leaned on my dad and he hadn't exactly proved himself to be a sturdy stake. I'd decided right from the start I was going to stand tall by myself, so I was surprised by how good it felt to be held like this. I had to confess it made me feel safe, which made no sense at all because why would I suddenly feel safe when I hadn't ever felt unsafe?

He pushed my tousled hair away from my face and tilted my chin so that I was forced to look at him. What I saw there made my heart bump hard. I'd got so used to thinking of him as remote and cold that the warmth in his eyes wrecked me.

'*Bellissima,*' he murmured softly and I didn't speak any Italian, but I knew he was telling me I was beautiful.

Sexual intimacy had turned into something else and nerves were jumping in my tummy when he lowered his head, delivered a lingering kiss to my mouth and then stood up. He picked up my discarded hair clip, handed it to me and then scooped me into his arms. I locked my arms round his neck because although he'd more than demonstrated how strong he was, I didn't trust him not to drop me. I wasn't used to being carried anywhere, but nothing about this night was normal.

'Why are you giving me my hair clip? Where are we going?'

'It's a surprise.'

'After that disastrous wedding I've gone off surprises. I prefer to know what's going to happen so I can prepare for it.'

His mouth flickered at the corners. 'We're going to the bedroom. I don't want you to get cold.'

Cold? Was he kidding? I was so hot that if he'd put a slice of bread on me I could have turned it into toast.

But it was evidence he didn't intend to end the evening yet, so I wasn't about to argue with his reasoning. And anyway, if I was honest, I was enjoying the cuddle.

I tore my greedy gaze away from the strong lines of his jaw to take a glimpse of his apartment. 'It's amazing. The view is incredible.'

He lowered me to the floor and I saw that his bedroom was dominated by—well, the bed. It was slightly raised and positioned to take advantage of the incredible views. Not that I expected to be looking at anything except him.

I pressed my lips to his shoulder. His skin was salty with sweat and he cupped my face in his hands and took my mouth with his. He coaxed my lips apart and kissed me and I was instantly desperate again.

I'd expected him to pull me onto the bed, but instead he took my hand and walked with me towards the window. I resisted.

'You really are an exhibitionist,' I began, but then he opened the glass door and I saw that there, on the deck with a perfect view of the River Thames snaking towards the city, was a hot tub.

'Pin your hair back up.'

It was freezing outside, snow still floating down like confetti, but he pulled off the cover and we slid into the hot water and honestly, it was the most delicious thing ever.

The guy knew how to live, I had to give him that. The heat seeped into my limbs and soothed. The scent was blissful.

Now I understood why he'd told me to pin my hair up. 'I love this part of London. Have you always lived here?'

'No.' Something about the way he said it made me glance at him, but his gaze was on my mouth and suddenly I didn't care if he'd lived here for five minutes or five years. We were both on a little seat under the water, my thigh pressed against the hardness of his. Far beneath us London was carrying on as normal, oblivious to our presence, and I wondered how the city could be oblivious to the amazing thing that was happening between us.

'It's a fantastic apartment. Where does Kiara live?'

'She lived here with me until a year ago when she started college. Now she rents somewhere with two friends. She wanted her independence.'

I was surprised he'd lived with his sister. This place had 'bachelor' written all over it. Perhaps she'd only moved in briefly. 'How long did she live with you?'

'Since she was twelve.' His voice didn't change, but still I sensed something different. Something complicated. I'd grown up with complicated, so I probably had a sensitive radar. And I was good enough with numbers to work out that he must have taken on that responsibility at a young age.

'No family?'

'Just the two of us. How long have you and Rosie lived together?' He was changing the subject, but I didn't mind. I wasn't usually mad keen on talking about family either, but for some reason right now, with him, it felt comfortable.

'Pretty much all our lives.' I leaned my head back and gazed up at the sky. Snow was still falling, light, feathery flakes that dusted my hair and his. I skimmed my hand over the surface of the water, watching as they melted. 'There's only ten months between us. We shared a room when we were growing up. They almost split us up, but we objected.'

'Split you up?'

'Dad walked out when we were eight. They fought over who was going to have us. All a bit crap if I'm honest. They thought it would make sense if each parent had one of us, but that didn't make any sense at all to us.' Rosie had once said it was like being the rope in a tug of war, but I didn't tell him that. Nor did I tell him about the time Rosie had hung on to me like a barnacle while dad had tried to pull her away from me and carry her to the car. In the end he'd given up. They'd never tried to split us up again, but Rosie had insisted on switching her ballet classes to karate just in case.

'Hence the "friend Christmas"?'

'Rosie likes to create her version of the fairy tale.'

'Your sister is very generous. She invited half of London for Christmas lunch.'

'Friends are our family.' I slid deeper under the water. 'What would you have done for Christmas if you hadn't come to us?'

'Worked.'

'So I distracted you. Sorry about that.' My voice was smoky soft and he gave a mocking smile.

'If that's your sorry look, it needs work.'

I lowered my eyelashes. 'Better?'

'No.'

'You want me to beg forgiveness?' I remembered I'd already begged and felt myself color. His eyes dropped to my mouth and I knew he was remembering the same thing.

'You're so sexy. Keeping my hands off you has been the hardest thing I've ever done.'

It was so not what I'd expected him to say I almost sank under the water. 'Really?'

His eyes gleamed with incredulity. 'You have to know that, Hayley.'

'Er—no. Why would I know that? You've barely ever spoken to me.'

'Exactly.' There was a hint of exasperation in his voice, as if we were talking about something that should have been obvious.

I thought about what Rosie had said on Christmas Eve. 'So if you felt that way, why didn't you ever talk to me?'

'You were with Charlie.'

'And I don't even know why.' I slid deeper in the water, forcing myself to think about stuff I'd avoided. 'Rosie and I have never been very good at relationships. Charlie seemed like the stable, traditional type. I suppose part of me thought if I was going to make a relationship work with anyone, it would be with someone like him.'

'Someone who would ignore the person you really are and sleep with your friend?'

'Thanks for reminding me.' I didn't even think of Cressida as a friend any more. Friends didn't do that.

'Does it hurt?'

I skimmed my hand over the surface of the water. 'No. Not any more. And if I'm honest, it was only ever my pride that hurt. I should have been heartbroken, but I wasn't. I suppose that should tell me something. Honestly, I'm just rubbish at relationships. My

New Year's resolution is to have emotionless sex. That's why I'm here.'

'Right.' The way he was looking at me made my cheeks burn.

'You haven't told me what happened after I left the wedding.'

'I had to arrange a fleet of ambulances to transport all the men who had heart attacks.'

'Don't.' I shrank at the thought. 'I honestly don't think I can ever show my face in daylight again.'

'No one was looking at your face, so you're fine.'

I laughed, surprised by how easy it was to talk to him. It was like removing a pile of rocks from a river. Conversation just flowed, held back for too long.

'I haven't thanked you for rescuing me. Everyone else just stood there gawping. Even Rosie was useless. If it hadn't been for you, I'd still be standing there like a Playboy centerfold. You were very quick on your feet. What happened during the speeches?'

'Having seen your impressive breasts, Cressida was in a foul mood for the rest of the wedding, but it served her right for stealing your man in the first place.'

'I'm glad she stole him. If she hadn't, I wouldn't be here now.'

'Yes, you would. It was always going to happen.'

My stomach flipped. 'It was? How do you know?'

'Because I was going to make it happen.' Droplets of water clung to his shoulders. 'I was just waiting for you to come to your senses and realise he wasn't going to make you happy.'

'You were?'

'I was hoping you'd make that decision, not him. When *he* made it I was worried you hadn't had time to come to that conclusion yourself and that he'd hurt you.'

I thought about my job promotion party when Charlie had got drunk and not even offered congratulations. 'I suppose I hate giving up on things. It feels like failure. Anyway, it won't happen again. No more relationships for me. Just crazy sex. More of this. I didn't know this was going to happen. I didn't know Rosie had invited you.'

'I know. That was obvious when I walked into the kitchen and saw your face.'

I turned my head and looked at him. 'I'm glad she did.'

'So am I.' He leaned towards me, his gaze on my mouth. His hand slid between my thighs. It wasn't that long since he'd been inside me, but I desperately wanted him there again.

I lifted myself out of the water briefly—very briefly because the blast of freezing air over my shoulders was

enough to convince me that under the water was better than out of it—and straddled him. I slid down so
that my shoulders were under the water and saw he was
watching me with that sexy, hooded gaze that made
me want to do wicked things to him.

'You are the best Christmas present I've ever had—' I
murmured the words against his lips and felt him smile.
His hands were locked on my hips, preventing me from
moving. His eyes glittered and his jaw was clenched.

'Let's go back inside.'

'Now?'

'Yes, right now. I want to see you. All of you, and
I can't do that without giving you frostbite.' With his
arm around me, he lifted us both out of the water and
steadied me while he grabbed a towel.

CHAPTER EIGHT

WE LEFT DAMP footprints on his bedroom floor. He closed the door on the cold, the snow and the rest of the world and urged me into the master bathroom.

His arm was still around my waist, his mouth on mine and he reached out an arm and thumped a button on the wall, sending needles of hot water over both of us.

Finally I understood the true appeal of a walk-in shower. We didn't have to stop kissing. Water streamed over my hair and down my back and I think he must have altered the flow or I probably would have drowned. He removed the clip from my hair again and it slithered down my back in a damp mass. His hands slid over my body, leaving no part of me untouched and I did the same to him until I thought I was going to explode. I wanted to open my eyes and look at him, so I groped for the wall and switched off the water. Steam swirled between us. I was standing toe to toe with him and I leaned forward and pressed my mouth to his skin. Droplets of water clung to his flesh and with hands and mouth I explored his chest, the flat planes of his abdomen, the power of his thighs. I took my time, licking him, tasting him and then dropped to my knees. There was only one part of him I didn't touch and I heard the breath hiss through his teeth as I teased him as mercilessly as he'd teased me. I came close several times, sliding my tongue over his warm skin, tantalizingly close to the hard length of him. In fairness I was willing to bet I was as desperate as he was.

'*Cristo*, Hayley—'

I glanced up and saw his eyes, inky dark and focused on me. A muscle flickered in his lean jaw. He was right on the edge of control and I kept him there for a moment, just to show I could prolong gratification if I had to. That I could match everything he did to me.

Of course I didn't last as long as he had.

I slid my tongue over him and then took him in my mouth, inch by glorious smooth, pulsing inch and I heard him groan something in Italian and felt his fingers lock in my hair. I wondered how I could ever have thought him icy cold. He was raw Italian passion—it was just that he managed to conceal it in public and I loved that. I loved that I knew a part of him others didn't. That he was like this only with me. I saw the *real* Nico Rossi. I preferred that version. More human. Hotter in every way. I used my lips and tongue, sucked and licked until he hauled me to my feet and pressed me back against the smooth, damp wall of his wet room, his eyes fierce and his breathing uneven.

I was breathless, desperate, but nothing compared to him. His eyes were fierce and he slammed his arms either side of me, caging me. Not that I needed to be caged. I wasn't going anywhere. I could feel the cool, smooth tiles pressing against my back and the hard heat of his body. It was the best kind of trapped I'd ever felt.

Water clung to his forehead and turned his inky dark lashes to spikes. He was the hottest man I'd ever laid eyes on and I hooked my leg behind his hips, pressing him closer, not wanting any space between us. He lifted me easily and I wrapped my legs around him and my arms around his neck. Heat throbbed between us and his first thrust into my body made me cry out.

'You feel incredible—' His voice was raw, but at least he could still speak.

I was incapable of making any sound that wasn't an animal moan and I simply clung to his wide shoulders, kissing him as he drove into me. We came together in a simultaneous rush of ecstasy.

He lowered me gently to the floor, but didn't let me go, which was a good thing because my legs were like jelly.

The room was steamy and warm, presumably from the heat of the shower, but to be honest it could have been from us.

Still with his arm around me, he reached for another towel—he seemed to have an endless supply—wrapped it around me, kissed me gently on the mouth and led me through to the bedroom. My hair hung in a damp mass past my shoulders and he dried it carefully and then dropped the towel on the floor without looking at it. He was looking at me.

One thing I knew for sure—if this was emotionless sex, I was going to do it every single day for the rest of my life.

I knew it was late the moment I woke. The sun was blazing through the glass wall of his bedroom, bouncing off the river like a million tiny diamonds.

I rolled onto my side and saw the bed was empty.

Then I smelled bacon.

I sat up in bed and realised my clothes were probably still scattered across his living room. Feeling like a burglar, I walked into his closet and found a shirt. One of his perfect white ones. Smiling, I slipped it on and it fell past my bottom and over my hands. I rolled the sleeves back, raked my fingers through my hair and walked in the direction of the delicious smells.

He was standing with his back to me, but he turned the moment I entered the room. He'd pulled on his jeans but nothing else and I stared at his chest and wondered how I could possibly want to drag him straight back to bed after the night we'd spent.

I wasn't any good at morning-after conversations and I gestured towards the door, conscious that I was naked under his shirt. 'I should probably get going—'

'Why?'

I tucked my hair behind my ear. 'I thought you might have things to do today.'

'I have.' He flipped the bacon. 'And I plan to do them with you.'

'Oh.' My stomach curled. A night with him hadn't cured me of anything. I found myself staring at his shoulders and the lean, athletic lines of his body. He was the hottest guy on the face of the earth.

'Unless you think Rosie needs you?'

I watched the way his biceps flexed as he reached

for a plate. 'She's working today. Christmas Day is the only day of the year she doesn't train. But I should text her.' Dragging my eyes away from sleek male muscle, I wandered through to the living room. Light poured through the windows, reflecting off glass and polished surfaces. Outside the sky was a perfect winter blue and the sun sparkled on the surface of the river.

I found my phone, sent my sister a text thanking her for my Christmas 'gift', which I had no intention of returning for a refund, and then stood for a moment, distracted by the view, thinking about the night we'd spent.

'Coffee?' He had the sexiest voice I'd ever heard and I turned and saw he'd put two plates on the table and was now holding out a mug to me.

'Thanks.' I took it and curled my hands around the warmth, even though his apartment was a perfect temperature. 'I love looking at the river.'

'Me, too.' He hadn't shaved and his jaw was darkened by stubble. 'That's why I chose this place. Are you hungry?'

'Starving.' I hadn't eaten since the turkey and we'd done some serious exercise. 'So you can cook.'

'I cooked for my sister for years. She's still alive.' He handed me a plate piled with fluffy scrambled eggs and rashers of crisp bacon and I carried it over to the glass table by the window.

My stomach growled. 'If I had a view like this I'd never go to work.'

'You're not working this week?'

'Officially my department is closed until January 2, but that doesn't stop the emails.'

'You're still loving your work?' He sprawled in the chair opposite me and suddenly the view had serious competition. I picked up my fork, cautious about answering. Thanks to Charlie I was programmed not to talk about my work.

'It's fine, thanks.'

'I remember how excited you were when you got the job.'

And I remembered he'd been the only one to ask questions. 'It's exciting and the people are—' I broke off, reminding myself he was probably just being polite, but then I realised he was still listening and looking at me, not at his watch or over my shoulder as Charlie had always done. And because of that I found myself telling him everything I was doing, and the more I talked the more enthusiastic I was until I realised I'd cleared my plate and must have bored him rigid. 'Sorry.'

'For what? That is the first time I've seen you that enthusiastic since that first night we met.' And he didn't look bored. He looked interested and he asked me a few questions that proved he was as bright as he was spectacular looking. 'I'm pleased it's working out. So NASA isn't going to get you yet.'

I blushed, thinking about that awful dinner when everyone had talked about their hopes for the future and I'd confessed I wanted to work for NASA. Charlie had mocked me (I think his exact words were 'Apollo Hayley—God help us all'). It wasn't ladylike to be interested in rockets and jet propulsion (although frankly, since that hot encounter with Nico at the wedding I'd though of nothing but thrust, and not the sort taught by physics teachers.)

I changed the subject. 'Tell me the history of the tattoo.'

He drank his coffee and for a moment I thought he wasn't going to answer.

Then he put his mug down. 'We moved from Sicily to London when I was ten. My English was terrible and—' he dismissed it all with a shrug '—let's just say school was hell, so I stayed away.'

'Really? I imagined you being a straight-A student.'

'That part came later. Back then, I was out of control.'

I eyed the tattoo wrapped round the hard bulge of his bicep. 'So that was when—?'

'That and other things.' His tone was flat. 'I was sixteen when my father died and Kiara was taken into foster care. I argued that I was her only family and that we should be together. Of course no one listened.'

I put my fork down, knowing how I'd felt when my parents had tried to separate Rosie and me. 'What did you do?'

'I grew up. I worked out what sort of job would make sure I got Kiara back and decided I had to be a lawyer because they earned good money and knew how to argue.' His smile mocked himself. 'I went back to school and worked every hour of every day. I got a scholarship to a top school. I was a social experiment— kid with a brain but no income, let's give that a try.'

'That must have been tough.'

'Tough was seeing my sister in a foster home. But they were kind people and they helped both of us.'

'And you did it. You made a life for both of you.' I mentally compared him to my dad, who'd left us. 'You did a great job. She's confident and charming and thinks you're the best.' It explained the bond I saw and the respect she showed him.

'It was hard letting her move into an apartment with her friends.'

'Independence is a good thing. And I'm glad you did,' I said softly, 'or we wouldn't be on our own now.'

His eyes met mine and then he stood up and pulled me to my feet.

'Let's make the most of it.'

★ ★ ★

We didn't leave the apartment for five days. Most of that time was spent in bed having amazing sex, but also talking and laughing as we swapped stories.

I told him about the time I'd built a rocket in the kitchen and made a hole in the ceiling. He told me how he'd blown up the toilets in school using sodium taken from an unlocked chemistry lab.

I still couldn't believe how much this cool, controlled guy had hidden in his past. I was thirsty to know more. Favorite band, favorite drink, best place he'd visited... 'Tell me your most embarrassing moment ever.'

He rolled onto his side and looked at me from under those thick, dark lashes. 'I once went to this wedding where the bridesmaid burst out of her dress—'

Laughing, I pushed him onto his back and straddled him. My hair slid forward, covering us both. 'If that hadn't happened we wouldn't be here.'

'Yes, we would.' His hands were in my hair. 'But I was planning to make my move *after* the wedding, not during. I was going to persuade you to cry on my shoulder.'

'I'm not much of a crier.' I lowered my head and kissed him, my mouth lingering on his. 'You're so sexy. Say something to me in Italian.'

'Pizza Margherita.'

I giggled, but the crazy thing was he even managed to make *that* sound sexy.

My phone beeped. I ignored it.

'Say something else.'

'Il mio vestito è strappato.'

'What does that mean?'

'My dress has torn.'

And I was laughing. Laughing in bed with a guy I wanted to know more about. I wanted to know everything, and finally I reached across to read my text from Rosie: *five days in bed with the same guy isn't emotionless sex.*

And I stopped laughing and realised with a flash of panic that I wasn't supposed to want to know more. Emotionless, unattached sex should be exactly that, but somehow over the past five days I'd managed to form an attachment.

I was in trouble.

CHAPTER NINE

'THIS IS YOUR fault.' I stopped eating Nutella out of the jar and poked the spoon towards my sister. 'You invited him here for Christmas.'

'Yes. Christmas! I didn't expect you to go home with him and stay until Easter. I was about to report you to the police as a missing person. What the hell did you do for five days?'

I grinned and she rolled her eyes.

'Really? So he's even hotter than he looks. Way to go.'

I abandoned the comfort eating and slumped back against the sofa. 'I promised myself I was done with misery.'

'Sex with him was miserable?'

'No, it was incredible! But now I can't stop thinking about him. Crap.'

And it wasn't just the sex I was thinking about. I kept picturing the way he looked asleep—those lashes shadowing his cheeks, strands of dark hair sliding across his forehead. I thought about the hours we'd spent talking. The things I'd told him. Things I hadn't told anyone else.

I'd discovered intimacy wasn't just about getting naked with someone.

Bathed in panic, I sprang to my feet. 'It was supposed to be just sex. Emotionless sex.'

'Right. Emotionless sex that lasted five days.'

I paced across the living room and then turned to her, desperate. 'What am I going to do? I need to forget him straight away and move on.'

'Is that really what you want?'

'Absolutely. Definitely. No emotional involvement.' I didn't tell her I was worried I was too late for that, but she probably knew because she stared at me for a moment and then sighed.

'OK, well, the good news is that it isn't New Year for another six hours, so you haven't blown your resolution. You can start fresh at one minute past midnight. I've got VIP tickets to The Skyline. Tonight we are going to party.'

'The Skyline?' It was my turn to stare. 'How did you manage that? Their New Year's Eve parties are legendary.'

'I meet a lot of people at the gym.' My sister looked smug. 'We will have a great time and you can forget all about him.'

I knew I wasn't going to forget all about him.

I wanted to ask if she'd really forgotten He Who Must Not Be Named, but I didn't dare. 'Will anyone we know be there?'

'Yes, a whole group of us and you are going to hold your head up high and wear your favorite black dress because it makes you look fabulous.'

'Great. Let's do it.' I ignored the part of me that just wanted to be back in Nico's apartment. 'It will be my first public appearance since I exposed myself (I didn't count Christmas). Might as well make it high profile.'

I did love my black dress. It had tiny crystals sewn into the fabric and shimmered when it caught the light. I'd found it in a charity shop in Notting Hill, otherwise I never would have been able to afford the label. It was brand new. Still had the tags on it. The owner told me that the woman who had brought it in had fallen in love with it and bought it, intending to slim into it. Fortunately for me, she hadn't.

Rosie was right. It was the perfect dress for tonight.

I presumed my lack of excitement was caused by the prospect of meeting so many people who had seen me half-naked.

'We're going to get ready together like we always do, and while we're doing that you can tell me everything.'

And because she was my sister and this was what we did, I did tell her everything. How it had felt. How *I* had felt. And how I felt now, which was totally crap if I was honest.

Getting ready to go out together should have been fun. Rosie opened a bottle of champagne left over from Christmas, but it reminded me so much of being with Nico.

'Are you nearly ready?' My sister was wearing a velvet skater dress with mesh at the sides and no back that looked perfect on her toned body. Her blonde hair was loose around her shoulders, a little messy, but that made it all the sexier. She wore a pair of vertiginous heels on the ends of those incredible, kick-boxing legs.

I blinked. 'Wow.'

'Wow yourself.' She eyed me and smiled. 'I predict emotionless sex will begin at five seconds past midnight. Let's go. The cab is here.'

I wished I could have felt more excited about the night ahead. It might have been easier had the cab not taken the exact route along the river Nico had taken when he'd driven me to his apartment on Christmas Day.

'This is where he lives.'

'In Chelsea?' Rosie craned her neck. 'Colour me impressed.'

She would have been even more impressed if she'd known how hard he'd worked to get to this point and all the sacrifices he'd made for his sister, but I wasn't ready to talk about any of it. Nor was I supposed to be talking about Nico.

We arrived at The Skyline and took the glass elevator to the top floor.

The views of London were incredible and everyone was in a party mood. Everyone except me.

Rosie handed our coats over and frowned at me. 'You OK?'

'Great!'

We saw a crowd of our friends and joined them. The ones who hadn't accepted invitations to the wedding (because Charlie had alienated most of them) wanted to know if the rumors were true. Naturally when they heard that they were, they all wished they'd been there to 'support' me. Yeah, right.

'Nice one, Hayley.' Grinning, Rob put his arm round my shoulders and suddenly I was grateful for my friends. Friends were like shock absorbers. They made the bumps hurt less.

I saw Rosie watching me and tried to look as if I was having a good time, but of course she knew I wasn't.

'You'll forget him in time,' she murmured, handing me another glass of champagne. 'You wake up every day and one day you'll find it's stopped hurting.'

'Is that what happened with you and Hunter?'

Oh, God, I'd said his name. I'd gone five years without slipping up and now it had tumbled out.

I was dead.

My sister was going to kill me, right here on the dance floor on New Year's Eve.

I stood rigid, not knowing where to begin with my apology, when Rosie leaned in and hugged me.

'If he walked back into my life right now this minute, I wouldn't even notice him.' She whispered the words in my ear and then tapped her glass against mine and drank. And drank. And then helped herself to another glass and drank that, too.

I was about to point out that if Hunter walked back into her life now there was no chance of her noticing him because she'd be unconscious, but she slammed down her empty glass and grabbed my hand.

'Sister time. Let's dance.'

We loved dancing together. Considering what she

could do with those legs of hers, Rosie was quite re-
strained. Half the men in the room were looking at
her. Quite a few of the others were looking at me, but
I was glad to be dancing with my sister. To be honest,
I wasn't interested.

Then I looked up and saw him standing in the doorway.

Nico Rossi.

He hadn't seen me, but he was looking round the
room, searching for someone. He was wearing a suit. It
looked like the Tom Ford, only this time his shirt was
black. As always he looked smoking hot, even more so
now I knew how it felt to be with him.

An explosion of excitement and joy was followed
by blinding panic.

I didn't think I was up to seeing him spend New
Year's Eve picking up another woman and already I
could see heads turning because he was the sort of
guy who eclipsed every other man in the room without even trying.

I was in such a sorry state I didn't even realise I'd
stopped dancing until Rosie took my arm and hauled
me off the dance floor and behind a pillar.

'I have to get out of here,' I babbled. 'I'm really sorry
to ruin your evening, but I'm going home.'

The music was throbbing and pounding and I saw

her lips move, but I couldn't hear her and she rolled her eyes and dragged me out onto the terrace where everyone would gather to watch fireworks over the Thames at midnight.

'Breathe.'

'I'm going to grab a cab.'

'You are not leaving.'

'I have to.'

'Why?'

'Because—' I breathed and sent clouds into the freezing air. 'Because I can't bear to watch him picking up another woman. I can't bear to think of him with someone else.'

'And doesn't that tell you something?'

'Yes! It tells me I totally fucked up my New Year's resolution before the first chime of the clock!'

'So maybe you should rethink your resolution.'

I thought of all the pain and agony that went with relationships. The hope and then the horrible let-down. 'No. I'm just not putting myself through that again.'

'Through what? You just spent five days in bed with the guy. *Five days*. You laughed. You talked. He listened to you, which is more than Charlie ever did. He *likes* you for God's sake—'

'He's come here because he's looking for a date.'

'He's looking for *you*.' She said it quietly. 'Hayley,

this super-hot guy is walking across the room right now looking for you and you are *not* going to hide.'

'I'll mess it up. Look what happened with Charlie.'

'Charlie is a dickhead,' Rosie said calmly. 'You picked him because— Well, frankly I don't know why you picked him. We both know that when it comes to relationships our psychology is a bit warped, but he was totally wrong for you and Nico isn't. You two have something. Don't throw that away.'

'He probably isn't looking for me. I'm leaving and if you love me you'll let me go.' I winced as her hand locked around my wrist. Honestly, if the police ever ran short on handcuffs they could use my sister.

'I love you,' she said sweetly, 'which is why I am not letting you go. I'm not going to let you blow this.'

'I'm scared.'

'Yeah. I get all that. But it's OK to be scared, as long as you do it anyway.'

I thought about pointing out she hadn't done it since Mr You Know Who had broken her heart in two, but I decided that mentioning his name twice in one evening after five years of silence on the subject was a risk I wasn't prepared to take. And anyway, this was my panic. I didn't want to share it. 'He'll mess me up.'

'Maybe he won't.'

I'd never heard my sister sound so serious. 'What's

happened to you? You were the one who thought my New Year's resolution was a good one.'

'That was before I saw you with him.' She took a deep breath and smiled. 'If you run away from Nico Rossi then you are batshit crazy.'

I made a sound that was halfway between a laugh and a sob and saw Nico standing in the doorway. Those dark eyes were fixed on my face and he didn't glance left or right at the women who were staring at him hopefully.

Rosie released my wrist and my blood had a silent party, relieved to finally be able to flow around un-interrupted. 'Excuse me. There's a good dance floor going to waste,' she murmured and slid past him with a smile.

Nico nodded to her, his gaze still fixed on me.

There was nowhere I could go. I was trapped on the terrace and now I was shivering. It had stopped snow-ing, but the air was freezing.

He strolled across to me, removed his jacket and draped it around my shoulders. 'I thought you might be in need of a jacket.'

It felt warm and familiar and smelt like him. My tummy tensed. I was terrified I was going to give away how I was feeling. It had just been sex. I'd broken our rules. I felt like a snail without its protective shell, exposed and just waiting to be crushed under someone's heavy boot.

'What are you doing here?'

'I came to find you.' He sounded so sure and confident. 'There are things I need to say. Preferably before the clock strikes midnight.'

'Why? Does your Ferrari turn into a pumpkin at midnight?'

He didn't smile. He was too focused on me. 'I was ready to ask you out when you started going out with Charlie.'

Sound and people washed past me. I was oblivious to all of them. 'You were?'

'I told you I was ready to cross the room and talk to you, but I wasn't fast enough and for that I had to suffer watching you with him for ten long months. And then I had to watch you afterwards, coping with the fact he'd screwed your friend.' A muscle flickered in his jaw. 'Seeing you with him was like watching a car crash in slow motion. I just wanted to push you out of the way before you were crushed by it.'

'Nico—'

'He undermined you at every possible opportunity. That night in the restaurant when he put you down in front of everyone—' His voice was thick with anger and I wondered how I could ever have thought him cool and controlled. With me he was anything but.

'He didn't like me talking about work,' I muttered. 'He found it boring, especially on a night out.'

'Hayley, you threatened him. He wanted to be with someone who made him feel bigger, not an equal. He put you down and instead of bouncing up you stayed down. He stopped you being you.'

It was true. 'But that was my fault. I was trying to make it work.'

'How can a relationship work if you don't like each other as you really are? How can that sort of relationship be anything but false?'

It was a fair question. 'I was surprised you agreed to be his best man.'

'Why do you think I did that, Hayley?' There was something in his voice I didn't understand. An urgency that made no sense. 'Charlie and I have barely spoken since that night he got drunk and I drove you home.'

'Then why—'

'I agreed because he told me you were a bridesmaid. At first I didn't believe him. I couldn't *believe* they'd asked you to do that and I couldn't believe you'd agreed.'

I shifted awkwardly. 'You were worried I'd screw it up for them?'

'No. I was worried you'd be very hurt.' His jaw was tight. 'I was worried you'd fall apart at the wedding and need someone to look out for you. I was there because of you.'

I felt a lump in my throat. 'Me?'

'You asked why I agreed to be best man. That's why. You were the reason.'

'You—' I gulped. 'You kept looking at me throughout the ceremony. I thought you disapproved.'

'*Cristo*—' He dragged his fingers through his hair, exasperated. 'I was watching you to make sure you were all right. How could you not have known that? I was afraid you would fall apart.'

'I fell apart in a big way.'

'I must admit I hadn't expected it to be quite that literal.' His eyes gleamed. 'You looked so horrified I just wanted to get you out of there.'

'I've been checking YouTube for the video,' I confessed. 'There has to be one.'

'There was. But no one is going to upload it, I made sure of that.'

'You did? How?'

He stroked his thumb slowly over my lower lip. 'Let's just say I used lawyerly intimidation.'

I felt weak with relief. 'I knew there had to be a reason why no one had posted it. I had no idea it was you. You—you said I made bad decisions.'

'Dating Charlie was a bad decision. Agreeing to be their bridesmaid was worse.'

And I'd had no idea that was how he felt. But suddenly I was seeing it all differently. The way Rosie had seen it. 'You were always there when I needed someone. You gave me your jacket, you drove me home when Charlie was drunk and acted like a dickhead, you gave me multiple orgasms when I thought I was going to die of frustration—'

'I want so much more than your thanks.' He cupped my face in his hands and my heart was pounding so hard I was surprised people couldn't hear it over the music.

'You do?'

'Yes. I want you. And I really do mean you—' His fingers bit into my head and his eyes were fierce on mine. 'Not a version of you I've made up to suit my own needs, but the real you. The you I saw that first night. The clever you. The you that knows about engines and wants a job with NASA. The you that can add up endless numbers in your head as a party gimmick. The you that loves llamas and would do anything for her sister. The you I've thought about every night for twenty months, three weeks and one day.'

I couldn't breathe. 'Nico—'

'The you that would turn up at your ex's wedding because you're too proud to tell him he's a bastard. The you that would wax a turkey and search for "The Niccolò" on your laptop—'

'All right, enough—' Blushing furiously, I glanced around, but everyone was too busy gearing up for midnight to take any notice of us. But I'd had enough public humiliation for one year, so I grabbed his hand and dragged him back inside into a quieter corner. 'My New Year's resolution was to have emotionless relationships. Just sex and hot men.'

'I know. But it's not New Year yet.' His mouth was close to mine. 'You still have about four minutes to make a different resolution. Do it, Hayley.'

I stared up at him and what I saw in his eyes made me dizzy. 'What do you suggest? And I won't give up chocolate and I'm not keen on ditching alcohol either.'

'How about giving up having relationships with men who want you to be someone you're not?' He spoke softly, his eyes gentle. 'How about starting the New Year deciding to be you and enjoy it? How about coming back to my place and starting the New Year as we mean to continue it—in bed, in the hot tub, together.'

It was as if someone had kicked my knees. I wanted to slide to the floor.

Everyone was gathered on the terrace waiting for the first chime from Big Ben.

Across the room I could see Rosie with the rest of our friends, all linked together, waiting for the count-down to New Year. We exchanged looks and she smiled. I knew she was thinking I'd be crazy to turn my back on something that felt this good.

I agreed with her.

I slid my arms round his neck.

'The last five days were the best time I've had. Ever.' I heard Big Ben chime and people started to count. My eyes were fixed on his. This felt like so much more than the start of a New Year.

'For me, too.' He spoke against my lips and I smiled.

'Do I get permanent access to your Tom Ford?'

'You seem to be wearing it most of the time anyway.'

The clock was still chiming. I'd lost count, but everyone was gathering on the terrace, bumping into us in their haste to get the best view.

A final chime, loud cheers and then an explosion of fireworks and the London skyline lit up.

Nico kissed me, slowly and thoroughly, oblivious to everyone around us and there were definitely more fireworks inside me than there were outside. Finally, he lifted his head. 'So what's your New Year's resolution?'

For the first time in a long while I felt like me.

Really me. I realised that this was my life and I could live it the way I wanted to live it. I didn't have to be someone I didn't want to be. I was allowed to have dreams and feel excited about my future. And I wanted Nico to be part of that future.

I smiled up at him. 'Let's go back to your apartment and I'll show you.'

★ ★ ★ ★ ★

Burned

Dear Reader,

Do you have a relationship in your past you think about? Ever wondered what would happen if that guy walked through your door again? Rosie, the heroine of *Burned*, is about to find out!

I first introduced Rosie in *Ripped* and the moment I hinted at a past relationship gone bad, I knew I wanted to explore her story in more depth. Karate champion Rosie has a close relationship with her sister and loves her job as a fitness instructor in a big city gym. She's a typical Cosmo girl, fearless and fun-loving and, when it comes to defending herself, no one has more experience than Rosie. She's been defending her heart since the age of eighteen, when she fell in love with martial arts expert Hunter Black. That relationship scarred her so badly she won't even allow his name to be mentioned, so when he walks back into her life, she knows she's in trouble and it doesn't help that the chemistry between them is hotter than ever.

Rosie will let him back in her bed, but will she let him back in her heart?

I hope you enjoy *Burned*!

Love,

Sarah

xx

CHAPTER ONE

HE WAS BREAKING up with me.

I shouldn't have minded. I should have been used to it after all the experience I'd had, and it wasn't as if I were in love or anything—do I look stupid?—but every girl likes to think she's irresistible and being dumped hurts, especially after the day I'd had at work.

There is nothing worse than every part of your life going wrong at the same time. You see the whole thing unravelling and you don't know which bit to grab.

'The thing is, Rosie, this just isn't working out. We're not compatible. You're not very—' he squirmed in his seat 'you know…'

No, I didn't know, but that was one of the things that annoyed me most about Brian. He never finished his sentences. He stopped before the end and I was supposed to guess the missing words. Of all the infuriating habits I'd ever encountered while dating, not finishing sentences was the most exasperating—and that's from someone who once dated a delightful individual who threw his beer bottle at the bin and missed every time, despite having perfect aim when glued to the Xbox killing aliens. I'm the sort of girl who reads the last page of a book first to check how it ends, so cliffhangers aren't for me. Just give me the bad news and get it over with. Don't make me wait.

I'd blown two weeks' rent on a dress and now it was going to waste. This place was expensive. Right on the river with a view across to the London Eye. I loved the London Eye. It was a fairground ride for grown-ups, a giant Ferris wheel on the South Bank that offered a perfect view of the city. The glass capsules made me think of a monster with big buggy eyes. I wished it would come and gobble up Brian.

I heard laughter coming from the bar area and saw a group of men, shirts unbuttoned at the neck, jackets slung carelessly over the backs of chairs, drinking champagne like soda. It was Friday night and they were office types with money to burn. Lawyers? Bankers?

One of them was watching me. He caught my eye and smiled.

I didn't smile back.

What was there to smile about?

The fitness club where I worked had been bought by a company I knew nothing about, which meant the job I loved was threatened. Who knew what changes the new management would want to make? There had been more rumours than workouts for the past few weeks and the uncertainty was driving me mad. And now my fragile love life had crumbled to dust. All in all it wasn't turning out to be my best week.

Feeling gloomy, I looked away and saw a couple laughing together, lost in each other. The man was handsome, the woman beautiful. His hand sneaked across the table and covered hers, as if he couldn't bear to not be touching her. Her eyes smiled into his. Their wine was untouched. So was their food. They were too wrapped up in each other to notice anything around them, especially not the girl being dumped at the next table. I wanted to step out of my world and join them in their shiny happy place.

Even as I watched, they stood up simultaneously, gazes still locked. I should have looked away, but I couldn't. There was something mesmerising about the intensity of their chemistry. I stared, fascinated, envious, as the guy threw a bundle of notes on the table without counting them. So cool. I've only ever seen that happen in the movies. If I'd done the same thing

I would have showered the table with receipts, expired discount vouchers, chocolate wrappers and a ton of other crap that somehow finds its way into my purse. He strode purposefully to the door, his hand locked in hers. I knew, I just knew, that they weren't going to make it to the car without ripping at each other's clothes. I'd never seen two people so into each other. Or maybe I had. Ever since my sister, Hayley, had got it together with Nico Rossi, the two of them had been like that. I was scared to open the door to our apartment in case I tripped over the pair of them in the hallway. I joked that it made me mildly nauseous, but honestly, I was happy for my sister. Neither of us found relationships easy. I was glad one of us had managed to find someone.

'Rosie? Are you even listening to me?'

I turned back to Brian, telling myself I wasn't jealous. Chemistry that intense was a bad thing. It could scorch a person. I knew. I was much better off sticking with this bland version of a relationship, even if it did fizzle out like a firework on a wet night. Better that than being burned.

'I'm listening. I was waiting for you to finish your sentence. You were telling me we're not compatible.' It was like one of those stupid reality shows where they're about to tell you who this week's loser is, who is going home, only instead of just doing it, they make you wait and wait against the backdrop of a drama drum roll until the whole nation is yelling, 'For fuck's sake, get on with it,' at the TV. To kill time, I glanced round the room. Sleek black tables shimmered with silver and candles. We were surrounded by the low hum of conversation and the clink of glass. A roomful of people enjoying an evening. People who were in relationships.

And then there was me.

Rosie the rejected.

I could hold water in my hands longer than I could hold a man. Not that I wanted a long relationship but hanging on to him until the end of dinner would have been confidence building.

'Look at you….' Brian waved a hand and I looked down at myself in alarm, wondering if I'd had a wardrobe malfunction. We're big on those in my family—just ask my sister, Hayley. But as far as I could see, it was situation normal. Same legs. Same flat chest. When my sister and I were dividing up the family DNA, she got the big-breast gene. Who am I kidding? She got the whole breast gene. All of it. I've always liked to put a positive spin on things, so I told myself a flat chest gave me a better view of my impressive abs. I'd worked hard enough to get them.

'I'm looking. I don't see a problem.'

'There isn't a problem! You're really pretty. Great bone structure, cute face, gorgeous smile and your legs are—' He cleared his throat. 'You've got *great* legs. Great body. It's not the way you look! On the outside you look feminine and fragile, but on the inside you're not….'

'I'm not what? Brian, for the love of all that is holy, *please* finish your sentences.'

'I did.'

'You said "inside you're not." What am I not?'

'You're not at all fragile.' His face was scarlet and the colour didn't suit him. 'There isn't even a hint of vulnerability about you.'

'You *want* me to be vulnerable?' I thought about the mess that lay in my past. I thought about my childhood, when I'd spent half my time feeling vulnerable. Looking back on how I'd been then made me cringe. And he was telling me he wanted me that way?

He finished his food and put down his fork. 'You're tough, Rosie.'

That didn't sound so bad to me. 'So is diamond. And it sparkles.'

'I was thinking more of Kevlar.' He sighed. 'You have to admit your interests are…unusual.'

'What's wrong with my interests?'

'Oh, come on!' His expression said it should have

been obvious. 'You're a girl and you like fighting. How do you think that makes me feel?' He glanced quickly to the left to check no one was listening, as if simply being seen with someone like me might be enough to knock lumps off his manhood.

I put my fork down, too. Not because I'd finished eating—being dumped wrecks my appetite—but so I wouldn't be tempted to stab him. 'Martial arts, Brian. You make it sound as if I'm pounding on people in the street.'

'What you do is violent! You kick people. You could kick me.'

I had to rein myself in.

I told myself it wasn't an invitation.

All the same I was tempted.

My shoes had a particularly sharp heel. They deserved a workout before they went back in the box.

A couple had arrived at the recently vacated table. I decided they didn't deserve to have their evening ruined. I glanced idly in their direction. She was pretty. Blond hair. Elegant. The man had his back to me but I could see his hair was black as night and his shoulders broad and strong. There was a stillness about him, an economy of movement that told me he could handle himself. I spent my day training with men strong enough to lift a small car with one hand, so there was no reason to give him even a second look but there was something about those shoulders, the way he held himself, that caught my attention. *Something familiar.*

My heart bumped my ribs and I felt a moment of sick panic and then I noticed half the women in the room were also looking at him.

I forced myself to breathe. He was a smoking-hot guy, that was all. Even from the back, he looked insanely good. Who wouldn't look?

It wasn't anyone I knew. Just some random stranger who had happened to pick the same restaurant as us.

'Rosie?' Brian sounded irritated that he'd lost my attention and I tried to forget about Muscle Man seated to my right. I didn't need a hot guy in my life. I had enough trouble with the lukewarm variety.

'Relax. I don't want to hurt you, Brian.' I was lying. Right at that moment I wanted to. Wondering what I'd ever seen in him, I sat back in my chair and tried to visualise fluffy kittens and other gentle soothing images to calm myself. 'We're supposed to be dating. Why would I want to hurt you?'

'I'm not saying that you do. Just that you *could*. And that feels a little weird, if I'm honest. A man likes to feel like a man, you know? And that thing you do…'

'That *thing?* Are you talking about Muay Thai or karate?' I noticed that the man at the next table sat a little straighter. I had a feeling he was listening to my conversation.

'Both! Whatever it's called, it's scary. I don't mind that you work as an instructor and a personal trainer—'

'Thanks.'

Detecting sarcasm, he sent me a swift frown. 'It's the fighting that's embarrassing.'

'You mean sparring? Competitions? Why is it embarrassing?'

'Let's say, for the sake of argument, we carry on seeing each other. Eventually I'm going to want to introduce you to my mother. What would I say? This is Rosie Miller—just ignore the fact that she's limping. She has the best scissor kick on the circuit.'

'I'm proud of my scissor kick. I work hard on my scissor kick.'

'For the record, the last girl I dated liked baking and book club.'

Baking and book club?

I stared at him, wondering whether to kill him now or wait until after dessert.

It was chocolate brownie, my favourite, so I decided to wait. I wasn't hungry, but no woman ate chocolate because she was hungry.

'Given that you're breaking up with me, let me give you some feedback here.' I leaned forward and pushed my arms against my sides to gain his attention—it was the only way I could produce any cleavage. 'Firstly, I am not interested in any relationship that culminates in meeting a guy's mother. Secondly, your manhood should not be threatened by who you date.'

'That's easy for you to say.' His desperation was coloured by a hint of sulk. 'We both know that if we were attacked, you'd be the one defending me, not the other way round. How is that supposed to make me feel?'

'Er…relieved?' I heard the man at the next table cough and I turned my head sharply but he was leaning toward his companion, attentive. I wondered if he was telling her she should join a book group.

'It makes me feel humiliated!' Brian hissed. 'All I'm saying is that it would be nice if you at least pretended to be a little vulnerable. Once in a while you could act like a girl.'

It was the lowest of blows.

He was telling me I wasn't feminine.

I felt the sting of tears behind my eyes and blinked furiously.

Why did I even care? It wasn't as if I thought Brian was my happily-ever-after. But happy to the end of dessert would have been nice.

And I had no intention of changing who I was to make him happy. My mother had done that and it had led to misery for all of us. I was determined to find someone who liked me the way I was.

Could the evening get any worse?

I sat there trying to catch my breath and then the man at the table finally turned his head and my evening was suddenly a whole lot worse, because it wasn't some stranger who sat there. It wasn't some nameless, faceless hot guy who a woman could fantasise about but never see again.

It was Hunter Black. Hunter, the first guy I'd ever dated. The first guy I'd slept with. The man who had taught me that a broken heart was more painful than a broken bone.

My nemesis.

His dark gaze burned into mine and suddenly I couldn't breathe.

Shit, *shit*.

I'd really believed I wouldn't feel anything if I saw him again. I'd told myself that if he ever reappeared in my life, I probably wouldn't even notice him. I'd walk right past, thinking he looked like someone I used to know.

I hadn't expected this gut-wrenching reaction. I felt as if I'd been hit by a truck and left in the gutter like roadkill.

Looking away, I stood up, scrabbled for my purse and knocked over my wine.

Brian cursed and tried to save his jacket and tie from the flood. 'Rosie, what are you doing?'

I was running. Running like hell. 'You're breaking up with me. I don't see the point in hanging around to watch the whole movie when I already know the ending.' I opened my purse and dropped a couple of notes on the table and, yes, a lot of other crap, too—I was probably the first person to try and pay a bill in old train tickets. 'As I threaten your manhood, I'll assume you don't want me to walk you home.'

Exercising supreme dignity and awesome balance, I strode out of the restaurant as fast as I could on those heels. My legs turned to liquid—not vodka, sadly—my heart was hammering and my palms were clammy.

Don't let him follow me. Please don't let him follow me.

And I wasn't talking about Brian.

I kept telling myself Hunter was with a woman, that he wouldn't just walk out on her, but that logic didn't reassure me.

How could it, when he'd once walked out on me?

Hunter did what suited him. If he wanted to walk, he'd walk. And if he wanted to follow me, he'd follow me.

I couldn't calm the feeling of panic or the wild need

to put as much distance between myself and him as possible.

I heard voices behind me and I was so desperate to get away I almost stepped into the road.

A horn blared.

I looked frantically over my shoulder and saw the group of men who had been drinking at the bar appear at the door of the restaurant. Apart from wondering why they'd left when they'd appeared to be having a good time, I barely spared them a glance. I was too busy looking for Hunter, still terrified that he was going to follow me, although why I thought that, I had no idea. I hadn't seen him for five years and he'd not sent me as much as a text, so he was hardly likely to be rushing to exchange news and phone numbers.

Relieved there was no sign of him, I dived down the alleyway that ran down the side of the bar and connected with the main road. Far ahead I could see lights as cars whizzed past, but here in the narrow street it was dark and quiet.

I walked quickly, heart pounding. What was he doing here? Was he back in London permanently? Did he live close by?

The questions ran through my head and all I could think about was getting out of there.

Hayley was at home. We'd open a bottle of wine and watch the latest episode of *Girls*.

Scrunched-up newspaper brushed against my ankles and I picked my way through the mess, wondering why people had to be so gross in their habits. A cat crossed my path, eyes glinting in the darkness, and I was trying to remember if that was lucky or unlucky when I heard footsteps behind me.

They came at me without warning. Surrounded me.

And I knew, cat or no cat, my luck had run out.

CHAPTER TWO

I TURNED, THINKING it was a good job my hobbies didn't include baking or book group, because these guys didn't look as if they wanted a cupcake or my tip for a good bedtime read.

There were four of them, the men from the bar, and only now did I realise that walking down this alley had been a mistake. I'd been intent on getting away from Hunter. I hadn't thought about anything else. For the first time in as long as I could remember, I hadn't thought about my personal safety.

'Hey, pretty girl, looks like you walked out on your date.' The one who had smiled at me took the lead. 'Good decision. Want to go someplace and have some fun?'

'No.' I said it clearly so there could be no mistake.

'I'm going home. Alone.' I checked out my options swiftly. I was halfway down the street, so there was no obvious escape and there was no other person in sight.

I was on my own apart from the cat, but he'd walked away with a disdainful flick of his black tail. You can always rely on a cat to do his own thing in a crisis.

I taught people to be aware, to walk away from a fight, and here I was slap bang in the middle of a risky situation. In my haste to put distance between Hunter and me, I'd broken all my own rules.

The second man stepped in front of me. He was bigger, heavier than the first guy, probably a little out of condition but his bulk gave him advantage and I could see from the glitter in his eyes he'd been drinking.

I stepped back, still hoping to walk and talk my way out of the situation.

'Excuse me.'

'What's the rush? Don't you think that's a little unfriendly?'

'What I think,' I said clearly, 'is that you should go wherever you're going and leave me to go where I'm going. And those two places are not the same.'

'Maybe they are, kitten.' The smile held just a hint of nasty. He moved toward me, pressing me back against the wall, crowding me, caging me. I didn't hesitate. I lifted my knee, power driving through my hips as I kicked him. The transformation from kitten to tiger caught him by surprise. He doubled over and I spun and caught him with my elbow. Shock gave me the window I'd been hoping for to escape but sprinting was impossible in my heels and I'd barely made it a few steps when two of them yanked me back. My head smacked against the wall and pain exploded.

Holy crap.

I'd lost the element of surprise and I was about to scream when Hunter emerged out of the darkness. His face was barely visible, his bulk menacing in the shadows.

'Let her go.' He didn't raise his voice, but I felt the man's hold on me slacken.

The guy I'd kicked was rubbing his leg. 'Walk away. This is nothing to do with you.'

Hunter didn't move. That might have surprised them but it didn't surprise me. He never had been any good at following orders. He'd grown up in a part of London that most people avoided, so a dark street filled with litter and city types who couldn't hold their drink was unlikely to elevate his excitement levels.

'I told you to let her go.' He stood dangerously still, powerful legs braced apart. He was so damn sure of himself and my stomach curled and my limbs felt like overcooked spaghetti.

That confidence and assurance had been irresistible to an underconfident eighteen-year-old. To me he'd seemed like a cross between a god and a guardian angel. I'd wrapped my shaky, uncertain self around him like a plant desperate for support, using his strength instead of developing my own. When he'd walked away, I'd crumpled.

It embarrassed me to remember how pathetic I'd been. The memory was so humiliating I tried not to think about it. I tried not to think about *him*. Deep down I knew he'd done the right thing to break it off—although I didn't think he needed to have been quite so brutal in the execution. I'd been so clingy, so dependent, so good at leaning on him I'd forgotten how to stand upright by myself. Never had a girl been so crazily in love with a man as I'd been with Hunter.

And I should have known better. My sister and I had camped out on the battlefield of our parents' divorce, and believe me, it was a bloody experience. We'd both graduated from childhood totally screwed up about relationships.

When you witness a savage divorce, it can do one of two things to you. Either you decide marriage is something to be avoided at all costs, which is what my sister, Hayley, did, or you decide you're going to do it differently. That was what I did. I was never going to make the mistakes my parents made, because I was going to pick the right guy.

And then I'd met Hunter and I'd thought I'd fallen into the fairy tale. Compared to him Prince Charming would have looked like a loser.

The man holding me let go of my wrist and stepped forward. 'There are four of us and one of you.'

Still Hunter didn't move. 'It's an uneven fight, which is why I'm telling you to walk away.'

I was the only one who understood his meaning. The four men thought the odds were in their favour.

I knew differently.

Mention Hunter's name in the world of martial arts, and everyone will know who you're talking about. His skill had been noticed at an early age and it was that skill that had won him championships and sent him across the globe to Japan and Thailand to study with the very best.

He had choreographed fight scenes for movies and appeared in a few. Not that I'd ever seen him on the big screen. I'd been trying to get him out of my head, so the last thing I needed was to be looking at a magnified version.

These four city types didn't look further than the suit.

They saw one man. They didn't see the power.

They came at him simultaneously and he unleashed that power in a series of controlled movements that had two guys bent over and groaning in pain within seconds and the other two retreating in shock. It shouldn't have surprised me. Hunter was respected, revered in some circles, as a strong, aggressive fighter and an inspirational instructor. But still, watching him in action made my stomach swoop.

I suddenly realised I was no longer being held.

'Get in the car!' His rough command penetrated my brain but I simply stared at him, frozen, because he was suggesting I go with him. For the first time in my life I understood the phrase 'between the devil and the deep blue sea.' And he wasn't the sea.

My teeth were chattering and I heard him curse softly. 'Rosie, get in the damn car. Move.'

I turned my head and saw the low black sports car parked at the side of the road with the door open. Was it really a step up to be trapped alone in a car with Hunter Black?

Without giving me more time to make the decision, he grabbed my hand and hauled me the short distance, all but bundled me inside and closed the door.

I breathed in the smell of expensive leather and elite super car.

Apart from thinking that Hollywood obviously paid well, I wasn't surprised.

Hunter had always been obsessed with power and speed. On my eighteenth birthday he'd given me a ride on the back of his motorcycle. I'd sat there, pressed against the power of the bike and the power of the man as we'd roared over London Bridge at two in the morning, realising I'd never truly felt excitement before that moment. It was that night, right there wound around Hunter's hard, muscular frame, that I'd discovered the difference between living and being *alive*. That was the night our relationship had changed. Before that we'd had hidden places. Secrets. By the time we woke up in the morning there were no secrets left.

After that everything had been a lot like that bike ride. Wild, exhilarating and dangerous.

I'd loved the fact that he knew me. Really knew me.

He slid into the car next to me and the doors locked with a reassuring clunk.

I hadn't seen him since the day he'd walked out and now here we were, trapped together in this confined space. I was so aware of him I could hardly breathe. The scent, the power, *the man*. The air was thick with tension. I could have reached out and touched that strong, muscular thigh but instead I kept my hands clasped in my lap and my eyes straight ahead.

I'd assumed if I ever saw him again I wouldn't feel a thing.

I hated being wrong.

I felt as if I'd been plugged into an electric socket. The air hummed and crackled with unbearable tension. He was insanely attractive, of course, but I knew that wasn't what was happening here. It was something deeper. Something far more scary and uncontrollable.

I wondered if it was just me but then he turned his head at the same time I did and our eyes met. That brief exchange of glances was so intense I half expected to hear a crash of thunder.

His eyes were a dark velvet-black and the way he was looking at me told me he was feeling everything I was feeling. How could a single glance be so intimate?

My heart was pounding. I wanted to get out of the car so I could work out what all of this meant.

I wanted to get home.

I waited for him to ask me where I was living so he could drop me home, but he didn't. Instead he pulled away and joined the flow of traffic. He didn't say a word. No 'How have you been?' Or 'I'm sorry I left.'

Just tense, pulsing silence so heavy and oppressive it was like being covered in a thick blanket. And awareness. That throbbing, skin-tingling awareness that only ever happened when I was with this man.

The restaurant was close to Fit and Physical, where I worked, overlooking the river. Usually I loved London at night. I loved the lights, the reflection of buildings on the water, the trees, the crush of people and the general air of excitement that comes from living in the capital. Tonight I barely looked at the city that was my home.

I heard a throaty growl and for a moment I thought it was the car and then realised it was him.

'Why were you with him?' His jaw was clenched, his tone savage and I glanced across at him, stunned by the depth of emotion in his voice because Hunter was the most controlled person I'd ever met. He was the original Mr. Cool. Not tonight. He was simmering with fury and right on the edge of control. I realised that the reason he hadn't spoken was that he was angry.

'Who I'm with is none of your business.'

'Why would you choose to spend your evening with a guy who thinks you should be doing baking and book club?'

He'd heard that?

I'd thought embarrassment was a split dress at a wedding—ask my sister about that one—but I discovered this was far, *far* worse.

Let's be honest. When a girl finally meets up with the guy who broke her heart, she wants everything to be perfect. She wants perfect hair, a perfect body, a perfect life. Most of all she wants to be in the perfect relationship so that he can see what he gave up. She doesn't just want him to feel a sting of regret; she wants him contorted with it. She wants to smile and admit that breaking up with him was the best thing that ever happened because it put her on this path to lifestyle nirvana. The one thing she absolutely doesn't want, especially in my case, is for him to have to rescue her.

I wanted to crawl onto the floor of his car and curl up there unnoticed.

I wanted to rewind time and spend the evening in a deep bubble bath with the latest issue of *Cosmo*. Most of all I didn't want to feel this way. The truth was I dated men like Brian because I didn't want to feel as if I'd been singed by wildfire.

'You can drop me here and get back to your date. I'll take the underground.'

'Because walking down a dark alleyway alone at night wasn't enough of a bad decision?'

He'd always been protective. He'd always tried to keep me from being hurt. The irony was that in the end he'd been the one who had hurt me.

'I travel on the underground all the time.'

'Not when you're with me.'

Heat flooded through me. 'I'm not with you.'

'Right now you are.' His tone was savage. 'And unlike your useless date, I'm not leaving you.'

'Why? Have you suddenly developed a conscience?' I watched as two streaks of colour highlighted his cheekbones and knew I'd scored a point. 'Look, I've never been one for reunions, so just stop the damn car and—'

'What the hell were you doing going out with a guy like him in the first place? He's not the right man for you.'

'You don't know anything about me.'

'I know everything about you.' His husky tone was deeply personal and I felt everything tighten inside me.

The chemistry between us had always been explosive.

I'd assumed it was because he was my first, but I was fast realising his ranking had nothing to do with it.

I stole a glance at his profile, wondering what it was about him that made me feel this way. He had the same features as anyone else: eyes, mouth, nose—his nose had been broken a couple of times. But something about the way those features had been assembled on him just worked. He looked tough, like someone who could handle himself—probably because he could—and the combination of rugged good looks and a hard body was pretty irresistible.

I felt a pang of regret that I'd wasted the time I'd

had with him. Instead of just enjoying myself and having fun, which was what I should have done at eighteen, I'd been clingy and needy. Part of me wished I'd met him a few years later. Then we would have set the world alight.

But it was too late for all of that.

'Just drop me off and go back to the blonde.'

'You don't need to be jealous. She's a colleague.'

'I'm not jealous.' But I was, and I hated that. I hated the fact that he made me feel that way after all this time. 'Fuck you, Hunter.'

And I had, of course. If there was one thing we'd been good at, it was sex.

His knuckles were white on the wheel.

His head turned briefly and his gaze met mine again.

It was like the collision of two tectonic plates. I felt the tremor right through me from the top of my scalp to the soles of my feet and for a moment I was back there in the madness of it, my mind twisted by the ferocious sexual chemistry that only happened when we were together.

With a soft curse, he dragged his gaze from mine and shifted gears in a savage movement that made me flinch. 'You saw those guys looking at you and yet you just walked out and let them follow you.'

'I'm not responsible for their bad behaviour. A

woman should be free to walk where she likes without fear of being accosted by losers.'

'You put yourself in a position where those losers could have hurt you.'

'So you're saying it's my fault they behaved badly?'

He clenched his jaw. 'No, I'm not saying that.'

I kept my hands clasped in my lap because the craving to touch him was scarily strong. 'I didn't know they were behind me. I wasn't paying attention. I was upset.'

'Because that guy told you to learn to bake cakes?'

No, because I'd seen *him*. All I'd wanted to do was run.

I was a coward. I prided myself on being gutsy and strong and I'd fled like a rabbit being chased by a fox.

'I didn't see any point in prolonging the evening. I've had a long week.'

'Did you run because of me?'

'Oh, please....' Now I was doing a Brian, leaving my sentences unfinished, but in my case it was because I didn't want to tell the truth and I was a hopeless liar.

Hunter didn't bother inserting the words I hadn't spoken. He didn't have to. He already knew the answer to that one. He'd always been able to read me. We probably could have had an entire conversation without opening our mouths.

Keeping his eyes fixed on the road, he drove past the

Houses of Parliament up to Buckingham Palace and then drove through Hyde Park, headlights bouncing off trees and sending a shimmer of light across the Serpentine pond. I didn't own a car. For a start, I didn't have the money to run one, but in London there was no point. Why spend the whole day sitting in traffic?

Hunter reached into a pocket in the car and handed me a dressing pad. 'Your head is bleeding.'

'It's nothing.' A bit of blood was the least of my worries. I had bigger concerns, like the fact my heart was hammering. It didn't feel normal to me. 'I had the situation under control. You didn't need to help out.' I took the pad, ripped it open and pushed it against my forehead, wondering what else he carried in this car. I hoped he had a defibrillator, because I was pretty sure I was going to need one.

'If I hadn't arrived when I did, you'd be a crime statistic.'

'I was doing just fine.'

'Your balance was wrong. You need to watch the way you drive your leg. You're straightening too soon and losing power. You need a ninety-degree angle. You need to bend more. And turn your hips.'

I was trying not to think about my hips. I was trying not to think about any part of my body, especially not the parts that were near my pelvis. I was worried I was about to catch fire.

For a moment I wondered if I was the only one feeling this way and then I saw his knuckles, white on the wheel, and realised he was struggling, too.

'Why did you follow me?'

'Because I knew you were upset. I wasn't going to leave you alone in that situation.'

'Why? You left me without a backward glance five years ago, so it's a little late to develop a protective streak.' I thought it was hypocritical of him to pretend he cared about my well-being when he'd once left me in a million pieces bleeding. Maybe that's a little dramatic, but that's how it felt.

His shoulders tensed and I realised that, far from seeming indifferent, I'd just revealed a wound the size of a continent.

CHAPTER THREE

OH, CRAP.

The first thing our mother taught us was never to show a man you're broken-hearted. I'd virtually dropped the pieces of mine in his lap.

'What I mean is, I've learned to look after myself.' I realised we were in Notting Hill and felt unnerved. 'How do you know where I live?'

'There are some things we need to talk about, but first I want to check that head of yours.'

I wanted to check my head, too. What had possessed me to climb into a car with Hunter Black? Obviously I had a concussion. I needed a health check, or at the very least a reality check.

'We don't have anything to talk about, but I do want to know how you have my address.'

He didn't answer me. Instead he took a right and then a left into the leafy, tree-lined street where I lived with my sister.

Our apartment was on the top floor of a lovely brick building, with views over the rooftops toward Kensington Gardens. If you stood on tiptoe and stuck your head out of our bathroom window, you could see Prince Harry (only kidding, sadly). We were right in the middle of shops, restaurants and the market. I loved it. Of course, since Hayley and Nico got together—you probably felt the ground shake—I'd had it to myself quite a bit. I didn't mind that. It meant I could practise in the living room without accidently kicking her or getting yelled at when I knocked a lamp off the table. Normally coming home soothed me. Tonight I was officially freaked out.

'Good night, Hunter. Thanks for the lift.'

'Is Hayley home?'

'How do I know? And why do you care?'

'You had a blow to the head. I'm not leaving you alone.'

'I want you to leave me alone.' I was fumbling with my seat belt, fingers slippery and shaky with nerves. Turned out I couldn't even do that without help and I felt the warm strength of his hand as it covered mine.

His fingers were warm, strong and totally steady

and it irritated me that he had so much control when I had none.

He leaned forward and his jaw, dark with stubble, was only inches from my eyes. I looked at the sensual curve of his lips and the urge to press my mouth against his was almost painful.

And then he looked at me and I knew he was fighting the same urge.

For a moment we sat there, the moment of intimacy disturbed by the flash of headlights from a passing car.

Mouth tight, he unclipped my seat belt. 'You're bleeding. I should have taken you to the E.R.'

'It's nothing.' I was struggling to focus, but it had nothing to do with the blow to my head. There was something about being close to Hunter Black that made the most level-headed of women dizzy. 'I'll be fine. Good night. Great to catch up with you again after all this time. Have a nice life.'

I never was any good at delivering sarcasm, a fact confirmed by his smile. It was a slow, sexy, slightly exasperated smile that acknowledged everything that lay between us. I didn't want to acknowledge it. I preferred to step over it with my eyes shut.

Desperate to get away from that smile, those shoulders, *the man,* I virtually scrambled out of his car and sprinted to the door.

'Stairs or elevator?' He was right behind me and I gritted my teeth. When I was eighteen, he'd left me at acceleration speeds that would have left his car standing, but now I couldn't shake him off.

'You've spent too long in Hollywood. We say *lift*. And you can go now.'

'Not before I've seen you safely home.'

'I'm home.' I didn't feel up to the stairs—not that I would have admitted that in a million years—so I stepped into the tiny lift but the moment he stepped in after me I realised my mistake. We were on the second floor. To be honest, it was crazy that we even had a lift in this building. The space was barely big enough for two people. It certainly wasn't big enough for two people who were trying to keep their distance. My arm brushed against his and I flattened myself against the doors.

It was only two floors but it felt like going to the top of the Empire State Building. Every one of those floors felt like twenty. Every second felt like an hour. I could feel his gaze on me and it took all my willpower not to look at him.

I was determined not to.

I wasn't going to.

I wasn't...

Crap.

I turned my head.

My eyes moved to his chest, to the narrow strip of his tie, the silk of his shirt and upward to the dark depths of his eyes. I hated him for walking away so easily, for not finding me impossible to leave—and I hated myself for caring so much—but that didn't change the fact he was spectacular. His features were intensely masculine, his hair black as the devil, cropped too short to soften those hard features. No one would argue that Hunter's hotness factor was right up in quadruple figures. And I didn't need to wonder what it would be like to be kissed by him. I knew. The memory was embedded deep in my brain. I hadn't been able to delete it.

I told myself it was the bang on my head that was making me feel swimmy. Anything other than admit it was him.

I hated him for making me want him again.

'It's good to see you again, Ninja.' The combination of his tone and the way he was looking at me made me feel as if someone had kicked my legs out from under me.

'I don't feel the same way. And don't call me Ninja.'

It made me think of the day we'd first spoken. I was sixteen and I'd lost a competition to a girl from a rival karate club. I'd been furious with myself, not least because I should have won. I would have, but I hadn't been concentrating. Instead I'd been glancing around the room to see if my parents were going to show up and embarrass me. They went through a hideous phase where they both showed up to everything, not because they cared but because they were trying to outdo each other in proving who was the better parent. In the end neither of them came. I probably should have been relieved they hadn't been there to witness my humiliation, but I wasn't. It just proved what I already knew. That neither of them cared.

I sat at the edge of the gym on my own, putting more energy into holding back tears than I'd ever put into beating my opponent, when Hunter squatted down in front of me.

I knew who he was. Who didn't? All the girls were crazy about Hunter. He was twenty years old, a skilled fighter, the youngest black belt our club had ever had and seriously hot, but he was too focused on training to be interested in a relationship, and anyway, he wouldn't have noticed me, because I was too young. Right at that moment I would have fast-forwarded time if that had been an option.

'Are you all right?'

I looked at him. 'I lost. I made mistakes.'

'That's the past. Next time you'll win, Rosie.'

For some reason the fact that he knew my name made me feel better.

'It doesn't matter anyway,' I muttered. 'No one will be watching.'

'I'll be watching.' He held out his hand and pulled me to my feet. 'Now go back out there, forget what's in the past and start fresh. Watch your balance. Keep your focus and concentration. Mistakes are learning experiences. Move on. Forget everything else in your life. That's what I do.'

I looked up at him, skinny, angular teenage me, and tried to imagine this broad-shouldered god having anything in his life he needed to forget. 'You have stuff you need to forget?'

He gave a faint smile and brushed a stray tear away from my face with the pad of his thumb. 'Everyone does, Ninja.'

Ninja.

I liked the name. It made me feel strong and suddenly I didn't feel like crying anymore.

He might have said something else but at that moment my sister flew across the room, school bag heavy with books banging against her hip. Her hair had half escaped from her ponytail and her breasts were doing their best to push the buttons of her shirt right out of the holes.

'Sorry I'm late. I had extra maths tuition and then Mum and Dad were arguing about where we were going to spend Christmas, so I gave up and left them. I ran all the way.'

My parents hadn't made it but my sister was here.

Hunter smiled at me and let his hand drop. 'Now you have two people watching you.'

I fell in love with him right there and then. Not because he was hot but because he cared.

There were a hundred other things he could have been doing, girls he could have been smiling at or flirting with, but he'd chosen to spend his time watching gawky, awkward, messed-up sixteen-year-old me in her karate competition.

From that moment on I no longer minded whether my parents turned up or not. I had Hunter. He was the one certain thing in my very uncertain world. He watched every competition; he offered advice; he trained with me. I knew he wasn't interested in me *like that*. I was just a kid. But suddenly I wasn't a kid anymore and on my eighteenth birthday he stopped treating me as one.

Everything changed that night, apart from the fact he still called me Ninja.

It was my nickname and it made me feel warm and special.

Hearing him saying it now was like having a knife twisted in my insides because it reminded me so much of that horrible messed-up time.

I felt the breath moving in and out of my lungs and I was holding myself still so there was no chance I'd accidently brush against him a second time. I could feel the heat in my cheeks and I stared at the wall even though I could feel him watching, cool and calm.

I stumbled out of the lift in my haste to get away from him, took the few stairs that led to our attic flat and had my keys in my hand when the door opened.

Hayley stood there. She was wearing skin-tight jeans and a top that emphasised the fact she'd inherited the breast DNA. The fact that her hair was loose and messy told me that Nico had been round. 'How was boring Brian?' Her voice trailed off as she saw my forehead. 'Oh my *God*, what happened? Only you can come back from a dinner date with a black eye.'

'It's not a black eye.'

'Did it happen at work? You need another job. Or at least a different hobby. I recommend astronomy.' And then she saw Hunter. She couldn't have looked more surprised if Mars had bashed into Pluto. Her eyes went wide and then flew to mine.

I couldn't exactly blame her for looking confused.

For the past five years I'd refused to talk about

Hunter. He was a subject we avoided. And suddenly here he was, dominating our doorstep.

I could tell she didn't have a clue what she was supposed to say.

She just didn't get it and I didn't blame her.

She sent me a look that said 'WTF.'

I sent her a silent transmission. *Play it cool.*

'I'm hallucinating,' she muttered. 'For a moment I thought I saw a rat on my doorstep.'

'Hayley.' Unmoved by the less than effusive welcome, Hunter placed his hand on my lower back and urged me into the apartment.

'She needs to sit down.'

I heard my sister mutter, 'She's not the only one,' and suddenly felt a flood of relief that she was here and I was no longer on my own with this. I'd heard people say how much they loved being an only child, how great it was to have all that attention. I'd never understood that. I couldn't imagine what my life would look like if it didn't have my sister in it. I was pretty sure it would be awful. I'd probably pretend it was great, because that's what people did, wasn't it? There were some things you were stuck with and some things you'd never admit to not liking.

Being stuck with my sister was the best thing that had ever happened to me (apart from the fact she ended up with the whole breast gene. I found that hard to forgive).

'What are you doing here, Hunter?' Hayley sounded so fierce I jumped, but Hunter didn't react.

'Bringing Rosie home. I need ice and dressing pads for her head.'

'I can sort out my own head.' Actually I couldn't. If I could have sorted out my own head, I would have done it long ago and I wouldn't have been so screwed up about him. When it came to Hunter, my brain was as tangled as the cord of my headphones.

'What happened to her head?' Hayley sounded furious. 'If you've hurt her again, Hunter Black, I swear I will donate your body to medical science.'

'That happens when you're dead. I'm still alive.'

My sister sent him a dark look. 'I could fix that.' She had her arm round me and was drawing me toward the sofa. 'Don't get blood on it. You know I'm a rubbish housekeeper and I'm still dealing with the coffee stain from last month.' My sister's idea of dealing with a coffee stain was simply to turn the sofa cushion over.

But I could tell she was worried and she paused for a moment, torn between the need to stop my head bleeding and a reluctance to leave me alone with Hunter.

Hunter didn't wait to be shown around our apartment. He found the kitchen, grabbed ice packs out of the fridge, wrapped them in a towel and brought them back to where I was sitting.

He was a good person to have around in a crisis. The problem was that in my case he was usually the one causing the crisis.

My sister tapped her foot. 'You should go now, Hunter.'

'I'm not leaving until I know she's all right.'

'Of course she's all right,' my sister snapped. 'She's with me. Who do you think looked after her when you walked out? I did. And you didn't exactly hang around to check on her, did you? So you can stop pretending to be caring. You left her in pieces.'

So much for my dignity. 'Hayley—'

'She cried every night for six months! She didn't eat. She lost weight. So don't think she's going to agree to start that whole thing with you up again just because you happen to have shown up in her life again.'

Holy crap. *'Hayley!'*

'She pretends she's over you—'

'I *am* over him!'

'—but she hasn't been serious about a man since.' My sister was in full flow, raging forward like a river that had burst its banks. 'She dates men she can never, ever fall in love with, which basically means she has a boring sex life, and no girl of her age deserves a bor-

ing sex life, especially when she's in her sexual prime!
Do you know what I bought her for her birthday last
year? A vibrator! And batteries are fucking expensive!
And it's your fault.'

Hunter blinked. 'It's my fault batteries are expensive?'

'It's your fault she gets through so many. You are responsible for that, Hunter Black. You and no one else.'

I was going to kill her. I would have liked to do it
slowly but as I was about to die of humiliation, there
was no time to waste. I glared at her, hoping she'd take
the hint and shut up but it was too late—Hayley was
in full protective-sister mode, firing on all cylinders
like one of the rockets that fascinated her so much, and
Hunter was looking at me with that smouldering, intense gaze that stripped me bare.

He was one of the few people, possibly the only person apart from Hayley, who had ever understood me.
There was a time when that had turned me on. Now
it was just a great big fat inconvenience. I didn't want
him in my head, poking around in my deepest, dark-
est secrets. It made me feel vulnerable.

I wasn't that girl anymore. I'd grown up. Sure, I had
a few scars, but who didn't?

As he'd once said to me, everyone had something.

'You should leave now,' I said stiffly. 'Thanks for the lift.'

He didn't budge. He stood there, those powerful legs spread, towering over us like a conquering warrior. 'Before I leave, I need to talk to you. There is something I need to say.'

Hayley pursed her lips. 'If it's sorry, then you're about five years too late.'

I was starting to wish my sister would turn into one of those people who never finished their sentences.

'There is nothing you need to say, Hunter. You were the one who told me to treat mistakes as learning experiences.' I closed my eyes because looking at him made my head hurt and my heart hurt. 'I learned. It's all fine.'

'It's not fine and you should definitely leave.' Hayley repeated my words like some sort of recording device. 'We know you're good at that because you've done it before.'

He stood there like Apollo, or maybe it was Zeus— sorry, Greek gods aren't my thing—his eyes on my face as if he was working something out.

Then his mouth tightened. 'All right. We'll do this another time.'

Another time? Over my dead body. This one time had been more than I could handle.

I was fast coming to the conclusion that reunions weren't for me.

As he strode out of our apartment, I waited for the click of the door and then flopped back on the sofa, on top of the magazine Hayley had been reading and the stuffed llama I'd bought her for Christmas.

Hayley flopped back with me. 'Holy crap.'

'Yes.' The llama was digging in my back and I pulled it out and flung it across the living room. 'What the hell were you thinking, telling him I was broken-hearted?'

'I'm sorry! I went into shock when I saw him standing there. My mouth and my brain lost the connection.'

'I know the feeling. Do we still have that fire blanket in the kitchen? I might need you to throw it over me to put out the flames.'

'He is hot, that's for sure.'

'I was talking about the flames of my embarrassment.'

'Oh.'

'What were you thinking, saying all those things?'

'I don't know! I wasn't expecting to see him. You could have warned me! You should have texted me or something. I had no idea Hunter was even back in London.'

'Neither did I until an hour ago.'

My sister thought about that. 'He is *smoking* hot.'

'He is not smoking hot.'

'Yeah, that's right, he's the scrawniest, most pathetic specimen of manhood that ever stepped over our threshold. It's amazing a gust of wind hasn't blown him over. Are you seriously trying to pretend you don't still want to rip his clothes off?'

'If I'd met him for the first time this evening, maybe. But we have history. It's all too complicated.'

'Only if you let it be. What did he mean when he said "We'll do this another time"?'

I pressed the ice pack against my head. 'Don't know, because I am never going to see him again.'

'But if you do?'

'I'll ignore him.'

She stuck her feet up on the arm of the sofa. 'He's even hotter than he used to be and that's saying something.'

'I don't need to hear that.'

'And you look great in that dress. He didn't take his eyes off you. The two of you have insane chemistry.'

'I don't need to hear that either.' Every time I thought about my embarrassing behaviour, I wanted to slide under the sofa—except you never quite knew what you were going to find under our sofa. 'I feel hot all over.'

My sister stood up. 'I'll get you that fire blanket.'

CHAPTER FOUR

DESPITE MY THROBBING head, I showed up to work early. I wasn't going to let an unexpected encounter with Hunter derail my life. He was my past, not my future. We had new management. We were now officially owned by the Black Belt Corporation. There was no way I'd risk giving them any reason to get rid of me. Hopefully, they'd see my bruised head and take it as a sign I was dedicated to my job.

My first class was waiting. As well as karate, I taught self-defence and I'd had the same group of women for the past year. We talked about threat awareness—I felt as if I ought to sit in on my own class after what had happened the night before—and I went through the areas of the body most susceptible to attack, in my case my heart, and demonstrated basic self-defence techniques. Sometimes I thought these women turned up only for the companionship, but I enjoyed the class and I liked to think if they ever needed to defend themselves, they might remember what I'd taught them.

Today as I got them into position for the warm-up, all they could talk about was some hot guy they'd seen on the way into the gym. This wasn't unusual, because the place was teeming with hot guys. As day jobs went, it was a good one, which was another reason I was wary about the change of management.

'Have you seen him, Rosie?'

'Who?' I tried to get them to focus but it was hopeless. The whole hour passed like that, with them exchanging giggles and asides. At the end of the class I sent them all off for a cold shower.

I had an hour before I taught my under-sixteen karate class, and as the new manager still hadn't asked to see me, I decided to use the time to train. After the night before, I needed to let off steam.

I started with cardio. All martial arts place a heavy focus on body conditioning. It's not enough to practice competitive fighting techniques. You have to be fit. Sometimes I run in the morning before work. More often I just find time in my day to use one of the gym or fitness suites. I skip a lot. And although it makes people like Brian shudder, the truth is the Muay Thai is a very effective workout.

Huge glass walls looked over the river in our main gym, so at least you had a decent view while you were punishing your body.

The place was half-empty and I warmed up and then focused on bag work. Because we used hands, feet, knees and elbows to attack, the bags were longer and heavier than normal punch bags. Muay Thai was called *the art of eight limbs* for a reason. Kicking, kneeing and elbowing a kick bag increased your stamina and power. After the fiasco of the night before, I worked on driving the leg in repeat kicks. If I hadn't messed up, I wouldn't have needed to be rescued. I was going to make sure it didn't happen again. But as I smacked my shin into the bag, I didn't pretend it was one of those four guys; I pretended it was Hunter. I was almost enjoying myself until I heard his voice behind me.

'You're straightening your leg and losing power.'

For a moment I thought I'd imagined it because I was pretending to kick him.

No such luck.

Hunter was standing there, black T-shirt and track pants skimming a body hard with muscle. There was just a hint of the dangerous about him and a self-confidence that had always drawn me as much as his looks.

Sexy didn't begin to describe him. My gaze locked on to his, blue on to black. I was out of breath from smacking my shin into the heavy bag and staring at him didn't do anything to calm my heart rate. 'What are you doing here? Are you stalking me?'

'How are you feeling?' He was looking at my head. 'Any aftereffects? Dizziness? Nausea?'

I had both those things but neither had anything to do with the blow to the head. Being in the same room as him turned my brain and my knees to pulp. 'I'm fine.'

He lifted his hand and pushed my hair aside so that he could take a better look. The warmth of his fingers brushed my skin and I felt as if I'd been electrocuted.

'What are you doing here?'

'I should be the one asking you that question. You should have taken the day off.'

'We've had a change of management. The last thing I need is to lose my job on top of everything else.'

'You wouldn't lose your job.'

'How do you know?'

His gaze slid back to mine. 'Because I'm the management.'

For a moment I thought I'd misheard and then I stared into those dark velvet eyes and knew I hadn't.

'Fit and Physical has been taken over by the Black Belt Corporation.'

'That's right. I own the Black Belt Corporation.'

'You?' It hadn't occurred to me it could be him. I felt stupid. I hadn't taken any notice of the word *Black* in the company name. But now I thought about it, it was obvious. Hunter had trained in this place. Spent every day here growing up. He'd loved it as much as I did.

And he was back.

Now I really did feel sick.

'You own Fit and Physical?' My palms were sweaty. I wiped them over my workout pants. I noticed he was wearing the same black T-shirt all the staff wore and wondered why I hadn't seen that the moment he walked in.

'I was going to tell you last night but I thought you'd had enough of a shock for one evening.'

James, one of the other instructors, walked into the room. 'Mr. Black—er, Hunter, could I just—?'

'Not now.' Hunter didn't even turn his head. He kept his gaze fixed on me and my skin burned as if I'd lain naked in the heat of the midday sun. My mouth was as dry as if I'd hiked through the desert. Once again I wished I'd saved this man for a time when I was better able to cope with him. I'd wasted what could have been the hottest, most exciting relationship of my life on my messed-up teenage self. I wished I could wind the clock back. I'd ignore the angst and enjoy the man.

James took one look at Hunter's face and then mine and backed out of the room, no doubt to spread the word that Rosie Miller was about to get her marching orders from the new boss.

I stooped and picked up my water. 'Right. Well, I'd better leave.'

'Why would you leave?'

Because I was about to leap on him, strip him naked and enjoy the sex without any of the angst that went with relationships. 'I think it's best.'

'Are you really going to walk out on a job you enjoy because we were once lovers?'

We both knew he hadn't been just my lover—he'd been my everything. Hunter had filled all those empty gaps in my life and when he'd walked away, I hadn't been sure I'd hold together. It had been like playing emotional Jenga. Once that all-important piece had been removed, the whole structure had collapsed. It made me cringe to think about it.

Fortunately, I'd rebuilt myself and I was pretty robust now. I wasn't going to blow over in a strong wind and I wasn't going to let the threads of my life unravel over a man.

There was no way I would walk out on a job I loved

just because working alongside Hunter reminded me of the most humiliating time of my life.

'I wasn't suggesting I leave the job,' I lied, 'simply the room. Unless you'd like me to leave the job?'

I dumped the problem right back in his lap.

Maybe he couldn't cope with working with me. Maybe he was afraid I'd revert to being that clingy, embarrassing creature he'd once known. I couldn't really blame him.

'You're exceptionally talented and I want talented people around me. That's the way to build a successful business. And we're going to grow this place into a successful business.'

The compliment robbed me of breath. So did his use of the word *we*.

I swallowed, wondering what it was about this man that turned me to a lump of quivering jelly. My skin tingled and my nerve endings hummed. I looked into his eyes and forgot where I was.

I was seconds away from doing something really stupid like kissing him when the door opened and another instructor put her head round. This time it was Caroline and the moment I saw the way she looked at Hunter, I realised he was the guy my self-defence class had been talking about.

Grateful for the interruption, I nodded and walked

past him out of the room, trying to come to terms with the fact that my dream job had turned to torture. I was going to have to see him every day. Work with him. And not kiss him. I'd had my chance with him and I'd messed it up.

I taught the rest of my classes on automatic.

All I wanted to do was go home early, but I had a late one-to-one with a lovely guy who had lost four stone and was determined to lose another two. He never missed a session, so I wasn't going to be the one who let him down.

As usual, I was the last one in the building.

I walked into the female staff changing room and stripped off.

I stood under the water, letting it wash over me. All I could think of was Hunter. I adjusted the temperature to cold, wondering how I was going to work alongside him without revealing how I felt. I was going to have to take a lot of cold showers.

I pulled on yoga pants and a T-shirt, left my hair loose and walked out of the changing room slap into Hunter.

He put his hands on my shoulders to steady me and I felt the strength in those fingers and the heat of his body. Awareness shot through me. It was as if my body was programmed just to respond to him, which was frustrating on so many levels when you considered I was working hard to convince myself that this was going to be fine. That my self-control was up to this challenge.

'What are you doing here?' I blurted the words out and he raised an eyebrow.

'I own the place.'

'Thanks for reminding me. For a moment it had slipped my mind.'

His hands were still on my shoulders. 'We should talk, Ninja.'

'Not a good time. I've got to dash. I'm meeting Hayley.'

Instead of releasing me, he tightened his grip on my shoulders. 'Are you going to spend the whole time avoiding me?'

'I'm not avoiding you. But I have a life.' A pretty boring, mundane life that was depressingly low on hot men, but that was my own fault. 'Have a good evening, Hunter.' I tried to move away from him but we were still toe to toe.

'I have plans for this place. Exciting plans. Want to hear them?'

I had plans, too. They involved getting out of here as fast as possible. 'Er…maybe later.'

His eyes were hooded. 'You're finding this difficult.'

'Not at all, but I'm already late.' I peeled myself away from him and tried to walk away but I had shaky legs and tripped over my own feet, or maybe it was his feet. Either way, I landed against the solid wall of his chest.

Oh, holy crap.

I heard him curse softly. Felt his hands grip my arms. Felt heat, strength and pumping male power. He smelled delicious and I closed my eyes for a moment, breathing him in. I looked up and my eyes had a close-up view of his jaw with its five o'clock shadow. The contrast between us had always fascinated me. His dark to my light. I was strong, but my arms were lean and sinewy; his were bulky and powerful and his biceps felt as if someone had pushed rocks under his skin. Being this close to him made me dizzy. I was so aware of him. The chemistry was electric, as if my body refused to pay attention to the messages from my brain. There was a tightening low in my stomach, a growing heat that spread from my core to my limbs.

And then we were kissing.

Not tentatively. Not gently. It was rough and raw. Hot and desperate. We kissed as if this were our last moment on Earth and we were going to suck it dry. His kiss was as skilled and every bit as exciting as I remembered. I felt the press of hard muscle through the fabric of his track pants, felt his hands cup my face as he focused all his attention on my mouth. It took one second for me to know for sure my teenage self hadn't exaggerated how this had felt. Two seconds to remember how it had been with this man. I was virtually crawling all over him in an attempt to get closer, but he held me firm and steady, his expert mouth drugging my brain, sending my head spinning in dizzy circles because Hunter didn't just take when he kissed—he gave.

I felt the thick ridge of his erection pressed against me, the hardness of his thighs, the solid strength of male muscle as he tightened his arms around me, kicked open the door to the changing room I'd just exited and propelled me back inside.

The door crashed back against the wall and I jumped. 'You'll be in trouble for destruction of property.'

'My property.' He growled the words against my mouth and I was wondering whether he was talking about me or the building when he flattened me against the wall and suddenly I couldn't think of anything but the way his mouth felt on mine.

My fingers were jammed in his hair. His hands were on my bottom, holding me hard against him. His mouth ravaged mine, hot and demanding. We were out of control. I knew it. He knew it. Neither of us did anything to stop it. Certainly not me. His hands slid inside my yoga pants. Heat flashed across my skin. I shifted restlessly against him, desperate for him to use those skilled fingers of his where I needed it most. He didn't. Instead he slowly drove me mad, stroking me with expert fingers, touching me with erotic precision until my hands dug hard into his scalp and I was begging against his mouth. I'd never been so desperate for anything. And then his fingers were sliding over me and inside me until finally I lost it. Pleasure exploded, hot pulsing pleasure, and I would have cried out but his mouth was on mine, smothering sound while his fingers felt every intimate moment of my release.

Somewhere in the distance a door slammed.

I heard him swear under his breath and the next moment he was hauling my yoga pants back up my shaking thighs and smoothing my tangled hair back from my face.

I didn't say anything. I didn't do anything. I just looked at him. And he looked at me.

He spoke first. 'I'm sorry.' His voice was thickened and his broad shoulders were rigid with tension. He was probably wondering what the hell he'd just done. I wondered if he was panicking in case I turned into that needy, clingy teenage version of myself. In fairness, that was the only version he'd ever known.

'Well—' my voice sounded husky '—that saves me

buying batteries on my way home.' I managed what I hoped was a seductive smile. 'Thank you.'

Without giving him time to respond, I scooped up the bag I'd dropped and walked jauntily out of the changing rooms—which turned out to be a major challenge on shaking legs.

Only when I was safely out of the building and on the street did I allow myself to react.

I leaned against the wall for support and closed my eyes.

'You kissed him?' Hayley handed me a large glass of wine. 'You were going to ignore him and somehow ended up kissing him? How did that happen?'

'Turns out I have no willpower. And it was a bit more than kissing.'

My sister was sprawled on the floor surrounded by papers. She'd been working all day and a light glowed on her laptop.

It was Saturday night and for the first time in ages we weren't going out.

We'd ordered pizza and eaten it out of the box, slice by glorious slice, wearing our PJs, because if you couldn't be bothered to use plates, you certainly couldn't be bothered to get dressed.

'So how was it?' Hayley sipped her wine. 'Pretty

boring and disappointing, right?' My silence must have
answered her question, because she leaned across and
filled my wineglass to the brim. 'You know your problem, don't you?'

'You don't need to list my problems. Brian already
did that. It's a good job we broke up or my birthday
gift from him would have been cake decorating classes.'

'Forget Brian. He didn't like the real you and every
woman deserves a man who loves her the way she is.'
She looked at me and I knew she was thinking about
Mum. Dad had known exactly what he wanted in a
woman. Mum wasn't it, but he'd married her anyway
and tried to mould her into the person he wanted her
to be. By the time he decided to upgrade, Mum was so
misshapen she'd lost her real self under the fake version.

'We don't always get what we deserve,' I reminded
Hayley darkly, and her cheeks dimpled into a wicked
smile.

'I'm getting what I deserve. Several times a night.'

'Thanks. I really needed to hear that.'

But I was pleased for her because she didn't find this
dating thing easy either.

Hayley was an engineer and men always found her
job threatening. Apart from Nico. He was the first man
she'd met who understood what she did. He found it
cool that she knew her atoms from her assholes. In fact,

they'd finally got it together at the wedding of the biggest asshole of them all—her ex.

'Sounds as if you just got what you deserved, too.
You just need more of it. I'm planning your birthday,
by the way.'

I felt a rush of warmth and love for my sister.

Hayley always organised my birthday parties. Not
at the beginning, of course. To begin with we'd left it
up to Mum and Dad because we'd been naive enough
to think parties were their domain. That all changed
on my ninth birthday. Some kids had entertainers—
we had our parents. Dad hurled one of my presents at
Mum (it was Cheerleader Barbie) and gave her a black
eye. I think my friends thought they were watching a
juggling act until Mum picked up the knife she'd put
ready to cut my cake. After that it got a bit real.

From then on Hayley had taken over. Usually she
talked a friend into holding it at their house so there
was less chance of parental embarrassment. And most of
our friends' parents felt so sorry for us they were happy
to co-operate. We were 'those poor Miller sisters.' We
were talked about in hushed voices with much purs-
ing of lips and barely concealed sympathy. We were fed
extra cakes and sugary treats as if an excess of chocolate
frosting and blocked arteries might somehow compensate for the fact we were emotionally starved.

They felt sorry for us, but in some ways we felt lucky.

We had each other and we shared a bond none of our friends had with their siblings.

In fact, it was my parents who were responsible for me taking up karate. When they finally decided to part, they were determined to split everything evenly down the middle. Mum got the bed, so Dad took the sofa. She had the cat; he took the dog. It worked so neatly they decided to do the same with the kids. She was going to have Hayley and I was going with Dad. We didn't much care which parent we lived with but there was no way they were splitting us up. I won't bore you with the details but let's just say they didn't try that again.

But I'd taken up karate just in case.

I looked at my sister. My family. 'What I really want for my birthday is a decent sex life.'

'Oh no!' She pretended to look alarmed. 'That means I'll have to cancel those cake decorating classes I booked for you.'

'You're not funny.' But I was laughing because the idea of my sister booking me cake decorating classes was hilarious. Not that I'm a bad cook, but you won't find me twirling cute patterns on the tops of cupcakes.

She closed the pizza box. 'Think of all those lovely comforting carbs you'd bring home every week. And you wouldn't want to eat them, which would mean all the more for me.'

'And then I'd make you work them off in the gym. You were about to tell me what my problem is.' I executed a perfect roundhouse kick, which probably would have looked scary had I not been wearing my cute bunny pyjamas. I missed my sister's head by the width of a pizza crust but she'd lived with me for too long to bother ducking. 'What's my problem?'

'Apart from your congenital need to kick me in the head from time to time? Hunter was your first lover. You built him up into this godlike figure and you've compared every man to him ever since.'

'That's not true.'

'It is. The two of you were really close. When he walked away from you, he tore you in two and you never even had a chance to yell at him, because he was gone. It's hardly surprising you're still churned up inside. You have so much unfinished business. And you haven't allowed any of us to mention his name for the past five years. In your head he's still the perfect man.'

That got my attention. 'He is so *not* the perfect man. That isn't why I hate talking about him.'

'I know. You're embarrassed because you think you were needy, but part of that was because you're romantic. You always were.'

I thought about what had just happened in the changing rooms.

I could have described it in many different ways, but the word *romantic* wouldn't have been anywhere in the description.

'You shouldn't feel bad about it.' My sister's voice was soft. 'Mum and Dad were behaving like idiots, but Hunter was always there. It's not surprising you latched on to him.'

'Please don't remind me.'

'That's all in the past. Answer me one question.' Hayley pushed the empty pizza box away with her foot. 'Who is the best sex you ever had?'

'My vibrator.' I said it flippantly but she carried on looking at me as only my sister can and I sighed. 'Hunter.'

'Right. You had amazing sex with him and you haven't had amazing sex since.'

I chewed my lip. I decided not to admit that tonight had been pretty amazing. 'And?'

'And you should have sex with him again. This time you've shaken off all the emotional baggage. It would be fun and you'd save a fortune on batteries.'

'No way. He's my boss.' Just thinking about working with him every day made me want to order another pizza. Ten inches—and yes, I'm still talking about the pizza—with extra cheese. And I'm not generally big on comfort eating. 'I wouldn't have sex with my boss.' Except that I already had, sort of.

Crap.

I wasn't sure I'd ever be able to use the changing rooms again.

Facing him on Monday was going to be a nightmare.

'I'm not doing this again. Not with Hunter.'

'Why not? You're not in love with him anymore. This time around, you can have the fun without any of the Romeo-and-Juliet drama. This time it's all on your terms. All the sex with none of the heartbreak.'

'I am not going to have sex with him.' I told myself what had happened in the changing room didn't count. 'No way.'

Hayley picked up the empty pizza box and stood up. 'Fine. Carry on dating guys like Brian, who isn't even strong enough to lift the cupcake he wants you to bake.'

'I don't judge guys by the size of their biceps.'

'Neither do I.'

'Just because you're having sex with an Italian stallion who has a brain *and* biceps, there is no need to be smug.'

'Do I look smug?' She smiled smugly. 'Take control. You're older. Wiser. You are working with a hot, sexy guy. It's a shame to waste him.'

'I'm not interested and neither is he.'

'You think not?' Her smile widened. 'For two people who aren't interested you generate a *lot* of electricity when you're in the same room. The two of you could solve the energy crisis with one touch.'

'I'm prepared to recycle and do my bit to conserve fossil fuels, but I'm not having sex with Hunter.'

CHAPTER FIVE

I TRIED TO ignore him, really I did. I ignored him so hard I walked into walls while trying not to look at him.

I took my classes. I trained. I attended meetings and managed to look focused and professional, which was more than could be said of the rest of the female staff, who spent their time with their noses pressed to the glass windows of whichever space he happened to be working in.

Hunter managed focused and professional, too.

But that's the funny thing about intense sexual attraction. You can try and ignore it, but it's still there. You can feel it on your skin. It simmers in the air, wraps itself around you, seeps into your brain and makes concentration difficult. I knew without turning my head when he was in the room, and not just because I couldn't get any sense out of my female clients.

And he seemed to be avoiding me, too.

Neither of us mentioned what had happened in the changing room that night.

Our interaction was all business. At least, on the outside.

A week after he'd arrived to take control, he pulled us all into the meeting room on the top floor of the building and told us his plans for the business. He talked about his vision. Unfortunately, he did it while wearing a karate suit and everyone else's vision was focused on his broad, muscular chest rather than his presentation. I kept my eyes on the floor but it didn't help. I kept remembering how it had felt with his mouth on mine and his fingers deep inside me. That sort of intimacy isn't easy to forget.

I shifted in my chair and caught his eye.

Shit.

I was glad I wasn't the one giving the presentation. I would have been stammering and distracted but Hunter didn't falter.

With the benefit of five years apart and some distance, I could see now why I'd been overwhelmed by him. Dazzled. I didn't feel like quite so much of a fool for falling for him. He was impressive. Self-assured, confident, self-reliant. All the things I hadn't been as a teenager. He'd been around at a time of my life when I'd been at my most vulnerable. It was as if something in me had been looking to supplement what was missing, to borrow what I didn't have myself.

I'd been looking for security, consistency and dependability because I had none of those things at home. Using our parents as an example, Hayley chose to reject everything to do with marriage and settling with one person. She became a lone wolf. But I'd always been more of a pack person and Hunter was a born alpha.

I realised now that as well as friendship and sexual attraction, there had been a lot of other things mixed up in our relationship. I realised we hadn't really been equals.

Things were different now.

I'd built a life I loved, my sister was my family and we had a great bunch of friends. True, my sex life was mostly battery operated but a girl couldn't have everything.

'Are you joining us tonight? Team night out. We're going to a club.' Caroline's mouth gleamed with freshly applied lip gloss. I turned away to avoid the glare, wondering if the extra shine was for Hunter's benefit.

'I don't think so.'

'Hunter wants us all there. He's really keen on team building. He wants us to bond.'

He and I had already done more than enough bonding.

I needed to keep my distance.

But Caroline was looking at me curiously and I realised that to not go would draw attention, so I nodded and decided to arrive late and leave early.

Like so many of my plans, that one backfired. Because I'd elected to arrive late, I found myself squashed in a booth, thigh to thigh with Hunter. He'd bought drinks, and everyone was laughing and enjoying themselves.

Everyone except me.

I couldn't think of anything but his thigh pressed against mine. I tried to ease away but James arrived, even later than me, and sat down on the other side of me, leaving me no choice but to move closer to Hunter.

My thigh was glued to his. I tried to ease it away but there was nowhere to go and I sat there keeping as still as I could, trying not to think about that night in the changing room. I stared at the dance floor and nursed my drink, wondering why on earth I'd agreed to come tonight.

Across from me Caroline stood up. 'Let's all dance.'

That sounded like a good idea but it turned out it wasn't. Dancing with Hunter, even in a group, did nothing to cool me down. I was so busy trying not to touch him I was barely moving. I was wearing my favourite red dress, which was actually little more than a stretchy tube. I loved it because it meant I could dance without fear of exposing myself, but tonight I wasn't testing its capabilities. The floor was crowded and someone bumped into me, sending me slamming into him.

I felt his hands close over my arms, steadying me, and I shut my eyes. I decided right there and then that there was only so much torture a girl could take.

Muttering excuses, I plowed my way through the seething mass of gyrating bodies and out into the street. I crossed the road to the embankment and hung over the wall, looking at the river. Lights sparkled on the surface of the water. I wondered whether jumping in would cool me off.

'Are you all right?' His voice came from behind me and I breathed deeply, knowing I couldn't show him how I felt. Not this time.

'Just needed some air. Go back inside.'

But he didn't. Instead he stood next to me and stared at the river. 'I didn't know you worked for Fit and

Physical until I took over the company and saw the staff list. I've made things difficult for you.'

'No, you haven't. It's no problem.'

'I enter a room, you leave it. When we're sitting next to each other, you stare straight ahead. We haven't talked about what happened.' His arm brushed against mine. He turned his head to look at me. 'I'm sorry.'

'Don't be.' I gave him my most sophisticated woman-of-the-world smile. 'You gave me a great start to the weekend. You're good. You always were.'

He didn't smile back. 'I'm not talking about the sex.'

'Oh.'

'You must hate me for what I did.'

Was that what he thought? I didn't know whether to laugh or be relieved he hadn't guessed the truth. If I hated anyone, it was myself.

'I don't hate you.'

A muscle flickered in his jaw. 'I walked out.'

'I don't blame you for doing it.'

'You didn't look pleased to see me the other night.'

'I was having a difficult evening. It was pretty frustrating that you just happened to show up when I was being dumped.'

'You shouldn't have been with him in the first place.' His voice was husky and sexy and I turned away to look across the water, hoping he couldn't see the burn in my cheeks.

'Look, what happened between us—that's the past. I don't blame you for any of it. I was a mess.' When he didn't respond, I turned my head and saw the shock in his eyes. 'What? Do you think I'm so lacking in self-insight I didn't know that? Hunter, I was terrible. Frankly, I don't know how you put up with me as long as you did. I was a nightmare. I can't even bear to think about it, because it embarrasses me so much.' Although it made me cringe to admit it, I actually felt better having said it. 'I'm the one who owes you an apology. I was like a piece of bindweed. I was a limpet and you were my rock.'

He breathed deeply and then lifted his hand and brushed his fingers over my cheek. 'You were adorable.'

No matter how hard I tried, I couldn't not respond to his touch. My stomach curled and knotted. 'I was needy, clingy and far too serious.'

He curved his hand round the nape of my neck, his thumb still on my cheek. 'I was afraid I couldn't live up to your expectations. I was afraid of letting you down. And I did.'

'We both know you did me a favour,' I muttered, 'even though your method was a bit brutal.' The most brutal thing had been accepting he hadn't loved me, but I wasn't going to say that. 'Forget it.'

'It was the hardest thing I ever did.'

I wasn't sure if knowing that made me feel better or worse. 'It's in the past.'

'Is it? Hayley didn't make it sound that way.'

'Hayley got a little carried away. She's my sister.'

'Whenever I thought of you, which was often,' he said softly, 'I knew you'd be all right because you had her.'

I wanted to touch him so badly. To make sure I didn't, I dug my nails in my palms. Then I put my hands behind my back. My chest thrust forward and I saw his eyes drop to my breasts.

For a moment neither of us moved.

I knew he was thinking about what had happened in the changing room. So was I.

'Do you know what I wish?' I spoke softly. 'I wish we'd just met tonight for the first time.'

'And if we had?' His eyes held mine, slumberous and dark. 'What would you have done?'

'I would have asked you to dance.'

'Maybe I would have asked you first.'

'You wouldn't have noticed me in that crowd.'

There was a long silence. His gaze dropped to my

mouth and lingered there. 'I would have noticed you, Ninja.'

We stood there, wrapped in the past and the smells of the city, bathed in the glow that was London at night.

I felt as if my skin were on fire. I was burning.

'Hunter—'

'Was it true what she said?'

We both spoke at the same time and I laughed nervously. 'Was what true?'

'Hayley said you hadn't been involved with another man since me.'

I shrugged. 'No, that's not true. But I learned not to take relationships so seriously. I went out. I had fun.'

'With guys like Brian who wanted you to join a book group and take up baking?'

I laughed. I couldn't help it. Brian was so obviously wrong for me it wasn't even worth defending myself and Hunter smiled, too, a smile of breathtaking charm, and in that moment I realised that no matter how much time had passed, nothing could dampen the attraction between us. It was off the charts. I'd never had this level of sexual chemistry with anyone, but I knew now it was my problem.

'We'd better go back inside.' I stepped away from him. 'You're supposed to be team building.'

This time around, I was in control of my emotions.

My feelings were my problem, not his. It was up to me
to handle them. To accept the truth.

He'd been the right guy at the wrong time and I'd
always regret that, but it was something I had to learn
to deal with.

CHAPTER SIX

IT WAS AN exasperating truth that the harder you tried to avoid someone, the more you saw of them.

I was determined to avoid Hunter as much as possible, so of course I bumped into him everywhere and it was very distracting. To be fair, the rest of the female members of staff were distracted, too.

I tried to work off my frustration in the gym. I took extra sessions and did extra workouts myself.

By Friday of the following week I was physically exhausted but nothing had dampened my sexual frustration.

I texted my sister, 'Pick up batteries on your way home.'

She texted back, 'Pick up Hunter instead.'

I ignored that, gritted my teeth and got on with my

day. I avoided the changing room because that made things worse.

I did pretty well until late afternoon when I saw Hunter in one of the studios, hunkered down in front of a skinny boy of about nine. I didn't recognise him.

'He's being bullied at school.' Caroline's voice came from behind me. 'His mum came in earlier in the week and talked to Hunter about whether he should start karate.'

We stood together watching as Hunter talked quietly to the boy and then gave him a lesson, one-to-one.

I could see the confidence flowing from Hunter into the boy, just as it once had with me.

'He's good with kids.' I didn't realise I'd spoken aloud until Caroline agreed with me.

'I guess it has something to do with his own upbringing. It's really important to him to help kids who are in trouble at home. It's kind of like a project for him. Probably because of his own background.'

I tried to remember what I knew about his background and realised it was very little. When we'd been together, we'd been so wrapped up in each other, so focused on ourselves, we'd rarely talked about other things. But as I stared at the tear-stained face of the boy—who was looking a lot happier now—I realised

I'd been the same. Older. Probably less endearing. But just as vulnerable.

A project.

I remembered that day Hunter had come over to me and wondered if he'd seen me that way.

Was that why he'd found it so easy to walk away?

Caroline glanced at her watch. 'We're all going out again tonight. There's a new club in Soho. Are you coming?'

I shook my head. I had to try and cure myself and the way to cure myself wasn't to carry on immersing myself in the problem. And anyway, I'd had enough torture for one week.

Instead I put my client through his paces and then decided to find a quiet place to train. I needed to let off steam. We stayed open until ten on a Friday, so I changed quickly and found an empty studio. I didn't bother turning the lights on. Instead I practised kicks.

I'm a black belt in karate—men don't usually want to hear that—but I'd taken up Muay Thai only a few years ago. In Muay Thai we generally don't kick with the foot. It's full of small bones, easily breakable. We prefer the shin.

There was a bag in the corner of the studio and after warming up, I started practising. The kick is the long-range weapon of Muay Thai and the most important things are speed and placement, so I focused on that.

I thought I was on my own, so when I turned, breathless, and saw Hunter standing there, it was a shock.

'Why aren't you at the club with the others?'

'Why aren't you?'

'I had a client. And I wanted to train.'

'So let's train.' He strolled across to me with that loose-limbed easy gait that made my mouth water and my stomach curl with agonising tension. As he walked across the room, I noticed he didn't bother turning on the lights. The studio was in semidarkness, the only lights coming from the glow of the city.

And now I was trapped.

I could hardly tell him the reason I hadn't joined them on their night out was that I'd thought he'd be there. I couldn't change my mind without drawing attention to the way I felt. It was my problem.

Dealing with it in the only way I knew, I turned back to the bag but he caught my shoulder.

'No. Full contact.'

In other words, he was giving me permission to kick him.

I wasn't about to object to that.

Thai pad training is a classic way of teaching attack

and defence techniques. It helps improve speed, mobility and reaction time.

In theory the pads absorb the blows and minimise the force but I wasn't sure there was enough padding in the world to protect him from the energy I was prepared to put into my strikes. I was handling a lot of pent-up energy.

I waited while he strapped on belly pads intended to absorb punches, knee strikes and kicks and then I started.

I didn't hold back but that didn't seem to bother Hunter.

He stood rock solid as I came at him, coaching me, making suggestions, occasionally demonstrating a better technique.

'You're overrotating on your kicks.'

'I am not.'

'Too much hip turn without the shoulder and arm torque.'

'Anything else?' I turned, fuming and frustrated, and he smiled.

'Yeah, you're cute when you're angry, Ninja.'

The way he said it almost cut me off at the knees.

'Don't call me Ninja.' *And don't call me cute.* The words hovered in the air unsaid and his eyes held mine.

Then he carried on coaching as if that moment had

never happened. He gave me some tips he'd picked up in Thailand and I tried not to look impressed even though I was. Training in Thailand was my dream. Secretly I wanted to sit on him and torture him until he told me everything he'd learned but I didn't trust myself to be that close to him.

When I'd exhausted myself kicking the bag, we did clinch work. Close-up training.

Believe me, you did *not* want to be doing that with someone you were trying to avoid.

Without looking at that dark jaw, those powerful shoulders, I slammed him with knees, elbows, and then we were grappling and he tripped me.

Holy crap.

I fell onto the mat on my back and he came down on top of me.

I knew from the hold he used that we were no longer practising Muay Thai.

His gaze was fixed on mine and then he lowered his head and kissed me and his kiss was more devastating than anything he could have done with the rest of his body.

There is nothing about this in a Muay Thai training manual. Seriously. Being knocked out just doesn't mean this. He devoured my mouth with his as if I was the best thing he'd ever tasted, as if I were a meal and he couldn't get enough of me. It was as wild as it had been that night in the changing room and somewhere in my blurred brain I realised he'd been holding back when we were together the first time. His tongue slid against mine and I was dizzy with the feel of him, the taste of him, the intoxicating heat of his mouth on mine. My heart pounded at an insane rate and any hope I had of hiding how I felt vanished. I wrapped my arms round his neck but the padding got in the way and I writhed under him, frustrated by the barriers between us.

He shifted his weight so he didn't crush me and then caught my face in his hand so I was forced to look into the fierce blaze of his eyes.

'Is this what you want?' His voice was thickened, his eyes darker than usual and I was so hypnotised by what I saw in those eyes I could hardly breathe, let alone speak.

'Yes. But just sex, nothing else. I'm over you.'

His eyes were dark as flint, hooded, slumberous. 'Right now you're under me, Ninja, which gives me the advantage.'

He had all the advantage, but I wasn't going to tell him that. This time around, I had myself under control. This time, he was the one right on the edge.

The only sound in the room was our breathing. Beyond the glass lay the river and the crush of people that came out to enjoy London at night, but here it was just the two of us. We were alone, wrapped by excitement and smothered by a sexual tension that threatened to blow my brain.

He eased away from me and hauled me to my feet. Then he reached to help me remove my pads but I stepped back.

I did everything myself now. Everything.

'I'm fine.' My fingers were shaking but I managed it and he watched me the whole time, those eyes dark and assessing, as if he was making up his mind about something. Then he strolled across to the glass and stared down over the river. He leaned his hand against the glass and looked down into the street and I saw the rigid set of his shoulders.

I knew regret when I saw it and this time I was determined to cut him loose. 'Look—maybe you're right. We should just forget it.'

'Is that what you want?' His tone was raw and he turned, his gaze burning into mine. 'Is that really what you want?' He prowled over to me until we were standing toe to toe. My skin felt sensitive and heat uncoiled low in my belly. The look in his eyes made my heart pound because I realised I wasn't seeing regret.

'I—well—' I was stammering, torn between the lie and the truth. I couldn't think with him standing this close. I couldn't breathe. I licked my lips. 'No. I don't want to forget it. I wish…' Oh, God, I was as bad as Brian, stopping in midsentence, but Hunter simply slid his fingers under my chin and tilted my face to his.

'What do you wish?'

'Like I said the other night, I wish I'd met you for the first time now.'

'Why?'

I gave a half smile. 'Because we would have had great sex. You're the only man I've ever met who isn't threatened by my turning kick. I don't scare you or threaten your masculinity.'

He lifted his eyebrows. 'That happens?'

'All the time. My turning kick might not impress you but it's a turnoff for some.' I tried to keep it light and suddenly I didn't feel like laughing.

The truth was I longed for someone who liked me the way I was. Who encouraged me and supported me while I travelled the route I'd chosen instead of always trying to push me onto another path.

Hunter wasn't smiling either. He lifted his hand and pushed my hair back from my face. 'I happen to love your turning kick,' he said softly. 'And you don't scare me or threaten my masculinity.'

I suspected that nothing aside from a direct hit in the balls would threaten his masculinity and possibly not even that. I'd never met any man as comfortable in his skin as Hunter.

He was silent for a moment, as if making up his mind about something. Then he muttered something under his breath and let his hand drop.

'So let's pretend we're meeting for the first time. Have dinner with me.'

It was the last thing I'd expected him to say. 'Why would I do that?'

'Because you want to. Because you've thought about me every day for the past five years.'

I gasped. 'You arrogant b—'

'And because I want to, and I've thought about you every day for the past five years.'

His words knocked the protest out of my mouth and the breath from my lungs.

It was like landing on my back on the mat.

I stood drowning in fathoms of emotion, trying to fight my way to the surface, trying to get my head above it so I could breathe.

'It's been a long week. I'm not in the mood for going out.'

'Neither am I. We'll go to my place.' His tone was rough and I immediately knew he was feeling the way I was feeling. I could hear it in his voice.

I stood for a moment staring at the door, knowing

I had to make a decision because both of us knew this wasn't about dinner.

We could carry on as we were, dancing around the past, kissing whenever we came too close, fighting it, pretending it wasn't happening. Or we could make an active decision. We could choose to step forward or back.

And I realised Hayley had been right when she'd said I'd never moved on.

I'd never had chemistry with a man as I did with Hunter. And maybe I was seeing the past through rose-tinted glasses, but I knew I had to find out. I couldn't go through life using him as the ruler against which I measured every man—and I was talking figuratively, in case you thought I went round sticking a ruler down men's pants.

I wasn't the same vulnerable teenager he'd rescued. I'd grown up. Last time he'd had my heart, but this time my heart was mine. All that was on offer was my body.

'How far is your place?' I was so desperate I wasn't sure I'd make it and he smiled as he held the door open for me, waiting while I picked up my bag and all my gear.

'One floor. I live upstairs.'

That close? My heart rate doubled. 'Upstairs?'

'You didn't know?' He walked down the corridor toward the foyer but instead of going down to the ground floor, we went up. 'I lease the apartment with the rest of the building. It has great views. We can eat and talk without being crushed by the Friday-night London crowd.'

I didn't think talking was what either of us had in mind.

CHAPTER SEVEN

HUNTER'S APARTMENT WAS spectacular and the crazy thing was I hadn't even known it existed. I'd worked at Fit and Physical since I finished my degree in physiology and sports science and I'd never once wondered what was on the floor above us.

The answer was two floors of real-estate nirvana.

The living room stretched across the whole of the building, open plan with huge glass walls that looked across the river. Cream sofas were grouped around an ultra-modern fireplace enclosed by glass and in one corner was a dining table positioned to make the most of the spectacular views.

'Nice.' I thought of our little apartment in Notting Hill. We loved it but you could barely do a scissor kick without knocking something over. Here you could

have held a tournament and still not filled the floor
space. 'It's huge. Who are you living with? There's
space for the whole of the British karate team.'

He gave a faint smile. 'Just me. I like space. I don't
like feeling enclosed.'

'Who lived here before you?'

'A banker. He moved out when I bought the building.'

'So Hollywood pays well.' I strolled to the windows
and stared out across the river. 'It reminds me of Nico's
apartment.'

'Nico?' His voice was a little cooler and I smiled. I
still had my back to him, so I thought the smile was
between me and the window but it turned out I wasn't
as clever as I thought, because he was standing behind
me and the window acted like a mirror. 'You're trying
to make me suffer just a little bit for what I did to you.'

'No. I don't play those games.' I could feel the
warmth of him behind me and watched as his hands
came to my shoulders.

'Who is Nico?'

'He's a lawyer. He's seeing Hayley.'

His grip on my shoulders eased. 'So who was the guy
you were with the other night? The one who wants
you to join a book group and bake cakes.'

'Brian.'

'What were you doing with him, Rosie?'

'Having dinner.'

'He's so obviously wrong for you.'

I could feel his hands, strong and sure on my shoulders. 'You're not the expert on me.'

'I know you.'

'No.' I turned so that we were face to face, so there could be no mistake. 'You *knew* me. I'm a different person now.'

'Why was he breaking up with you?'

'He finds me scary. Unfeminine.'

Hunter told me what he thought of that in a single succinct word that made me smile and then he slid his hands down my arms and suddenly I wasn't smiling anymore. I felt his palms, warm and calloused, brush against my skin. Knowing what those hands could do, I shivered.

I'd been badly burned, and here I was playing with fire again.

Was I doing the wrong thing?

My courage faltered. 'Maybe I should go. Are we being crazy?'

'No.' His voice was rough and raw. 'I really want you to stay.'

'Why?'

'Because I can't get through my day without thinking about you. Because I can't focus. All I can think of is you, naked and underneath me.' His jaw was tight, clenched, and it was obvious he was suffering as much as I was.

For some reason that made me feel better. Not that I wanted to suffer, but I didn't want to be trapped in this cycle of sexual torment alone.

'Who says I'd be underneath?' I shot him a look. 'Maybe I'd be the one on top.'

His eyes gleamed. 'Maybe you would.'

My breathing was shallow. I still didn't know what was going on in his head. 'I'm not some project.'

His eyes narrowed. 'What's that supposed to mean?'

'Nothing.' I decided this wasn't the time to think about it. It didn't matter anyway.

'I don't blame you for hesitating. I hurt you. I'm sorry for that and I'm sorry I made you wary about men.' There was a raw edge to his tone that caught my attention as much as the hard bite of his fingers and I realised I'd never really thought deeply about his reasons for leaving. I'd been so hurt all I'd thought about was myself.

I looked down at his hand, bronzed and strong, holding me firmly.

We could spend the evening talking about the past, going over what had happened like a tractor with its wheels stuck in muddy ground digging itself ever deeper instead of moving forward. But I knew I didn't want to live my life sinking into the mud of what had happened five years before. I wanted to put it behind me. I couldn't change what had happened, but I could choose not to let it taint my present. I could choose to be in charge of my future.

'It's history.' And finally it felt as if it was. I'd held the dream in my head for so long, held on to the emotions. I hadn't allowed anyone to mention his name, because I'd been so embarrassed by how needy I'd been, but I could see I'd been too hard on myself. Life had felt tough and I'd latched on to the person who had made it easier. Accepting that felt like a step forward.

I felt lighter. Stronger. More in control.

I knew who I was and what I wanted and I wanted him. Not because I felt vulnerable or needed the attention but because he was still the hottest guy I'd ever met and that seemed like a good enough reason to me. And it didn't matter what his reasons were, because I wasn't planning on letting my emotions in on this date.

I suppose we want different things at different times of our lives. At eighteen I'd been desperate for security. *Now?*

His hand tightened on my arm. 'Do you want me to take you home?'

I knew if I said yes, he'd take me to the car, drive me back to Notting Hill and that would be the end of it.

'No. I want you.'

'Are you sure?'

'Yes. But just for sex.'

His eyes darkened. 'Rosie—'

'I just want to be clear about that. I don't want anything else. I don't expect you to prop me up when I feel low, I don't expect you to hold me when I'm sad and I don't expect you to fight my battles. But we have chemistry—we always have—and good sex has been thin on the ground.' It had been nonexistent but I wasn't ready to admit that. 'I'm tired of dating guys I have nothing in common with in the hope we can have fun in bed. I'll just take the fun in bed and forget the dating.'

Hayley had done the same thing with Nico. Of course, that hadn't quite turned out the way she'd planned but I wasn't going to think about that now. I was different. It wouldn't happen to me. For a start, I was already immune. If you had a large dose of something, you usually didn't get it again. I'd already caught Hunter. I told myself I couldn't catch him twice.

'Can I use your shower?' I picked up the bag I'd brought with me and followed his directions.

'Help yourself to towels and anything else you need. I'll make us something to eat.'

It was a ridiculously intimate exchange for two people who up until a couple of weeks ago hadn't seen each other for five years.

I stripped off and stood under the water, aware of the water flowing over my naked skin. I couldn't stop thinking of him and I stayed under the water longer than I intended. It felt symbolic, as if I were washing away the past. When I joined him in the kitchen, I could see he'd showered, too. His hair was still wet. His feet were bare.

I was wearing my favourite pair of skinny jeans and a pink T-shirt. I wasn't dressed up, but neither was he. On the other hand, Hunter looked good in anything. Hayley was right. He was gorgeous. Smoking hot, and if I had my way he wasn't going to be wearing clothes for the rest of the night.

It was time to get Hunter out of my system.

Keen not to look too rabid and desperate, I slid onto a tall stool while he pulled a bottle out of the fridge.

I'd expected it to be wine but it was champagne and I jumped slightly as he popped the cork and then watched, fascinated, as he poured it skilfully without spilling a single drop and handed me a glass. His fingers brushed mine and I shivered.

'What are we celebrating?'

'Our first date.' His eyes gleamed and I grinned and raised the glass.

'Sounds good to me. So if this is our first date, you'd better tell me about yourself. Tell me about Thailand.' I sipped and felt the bubbles fizz in my mouth.

Hayley and I only ever drank champagne at Christmas, usually when someone else had brought it, and we usually managed to lose half the contents over the floor when we poured.

It tasted delicious.

'Thailand was both brutal and brilliant.' He cracked eggs into a bowl and whisked them efficiently while I watched.

He told me about his experiences training with the best and if anyone else had been talking, I would have been hanging on to every word because training in Thailand was a dream for me, but I was finding it impossible to concentrate. I tried focusing on his mouth but that didn't work either, because all I could think of was how it felt when we kissed.

I dragged my gaze from his mouth and watched him whisking the eggs. I didn't think that could be erotic, but turned out I was wrong about that, too.

There's something about a man's forearms I find really sexy, especially Hunter's. They were strongly

muscled and male. Dark hair dusted skin bronzed by
his trip to the Far East. He was powerfully built and
supremely fit, every inch of him hard and honed.

As he reached for the salt, I saw the muscles in his
shoulders flex. He must have felt me looking at him,
because he glanced across and his gaze locked on mine.

He stilled and I tried to look as if I'd been paying
attention to every word but I hoped he hadn't been in
the middle of asking me a question, because I didn't
have a clue what he'd said.

Slowly, he put the salt down.

My heart was pounding like fists against a boxing
bag.

We both moved at the same time.

I slid off the stool and he dropped the salt.

We collided in the middle of the kitchen.

I slammed him back and his shoulders crashed hard
against the fridge as he ripped at my T-shirt, tearing
it over my head.

'Naked,' he growled. 'I need you naked.'

I needed him naked, too, but I was beyond speaking.

His mouth was hungry on mine. His fingers bit into
my thighs as he pulled me against him. I could feel
the hard, throbbing length of him and his hands were
jammed in my hair.

It was rough and crazy. We were locked together and

my limbs felt as if they were melting. He lifted me and I wrapped my legs around him. He crossed the kitchen in a couple of strides and lowered me to the counter. My legs were still wrapped around him and I heard the raw rasp of his breathing as he struggled for control.

He stood for a moment, his legs between mine, his hands on my thighs trapping me. Then he lifted his hand and stroked my damp hair back from my face, his fingers lingering on my cheek. For such a powerfully built man, he was incredibly gentle. That probably shouldn't have surprised me, because martial arts is all about control and his control was absolute. And yes, that was sexy. There's nothing as erotic as leashed power and Hunter was all about leashed power.

I could tell he was fighting what he was feeling.

His fingers lingered on my face and he tilted my chin so I was forced to look him in the eyes. My stomach swooped.

I knew this was a turning point.

I knew he'd paused because he wanted me to be sure. He wanted me to have a moment of calm in this stormy, crazy world we created together.

Whether we carried on or not was my choice.

And it was the easiest choice I'd ever made. This moment had been inevitable from the moment he'd walked back into my life.

I lifted my hand and closed my fingers over his wrist, feeling strength and sinew. Then I turned my head and ran my tongue over his palm.

I've no idea what signal he'd been waiting for, but clearly that was enough, because he lifted his other hand, cupped my face and lowered his forehead to mine.

The anticipation was almost killing me.

The ache in my pelvis was so intense I had to struggle not to wriggle on the counter. For several seconds he just looked at me, and I looked at him, wondering how long I could keep this up without ripping his clothes off.

Just when I thought I was going to have to abandon dignity and beg, he slid his hand behind my head and brought his mouth down on mine.

This time there was less of the uncontrolled crazy and more of the deliberate. His kiss was slow, sure and insanely sexy. A strange weakness spread through me, the craving instant and total. If any man knew how to kiss, it was Hunter. I moaned and parted my lips against his, inviting more, offering more. Heat uncoiled deep inside me and spread through my body. My limbs felt shaky and useless. His grip on my face tightened, I felt the erotic slide of his tongue against mine and I lifted my hands to his arms, resting my hands on his rock-hard biceps.

I'd never been with a guy as strong as Hunter. Not that it should make a difference, because it's not as if he used that strength when we were having sex. On the contrary, he controlled it ruthlessly, held himself in check, but there was something about knowing he was doing that that was deeply sexy. He was all man, from the top of his glossy hair to the soles of his bare feet.

He curved an arm round my back, holding me firmly, and the other slid to my breast.

I wasn't wearing a bra, because frankly, there wasn't much point. The rough pads of his fingers grazed my nipple and sensation shot through me. Just a touch, a simple touch, and yet already I was desperate. The pleasure was dark and exciting, the intensity just a little scary.

He kept his mouth on mine, explored my mouth with ruthless control, but I could feel that control slipping. I could feel the change in him, feel the ravenous hunger that made his kiss a little rougher, a little harder and I didn't mind, because I felt the same way. Something happened when we were together. Something that, for me, had never happened with anyone else.

Without lifting his mouth from mine he dropped his hands to the counter either side of me, caging me.

I could feel him through the thick fabric of his jeans, rock-hard and ready. I heard myself moan and slid my hands round his back and under his shirt. My hands made contact with sleek male skin and rippling muscle. I ground myself into him, heard him curse softly and then he was lifting me off the counter and unzipping my jeans. It took a couple of attempts because his hands weren't quite steady and my jeans were glued to me but somehow that made it all the more exciting. I sensed that he was right on the edge of control and I loved the fact it wasn't just me who felt this way. And then I was naked, my jeans on the floor with the rest of my clothes, and he lifted me back onto the kitchen counter. I gasped as the cool surface touched my bare bottom. I was wondering what he had in mind when he straddled the stool in front of me. His eyes were dark, hooded and fixed on me. Holding my thighs apart with his hands, he finally broke eye contact and lowered his mouth to my inner thigh.

The contrast between the cold of the surface and the heat of his mouth made me moan. I felt his tongue trace the sensitive skin at the top of my thigh. Everything he did was full of explicit promise and my insides reached melting point in two seconds flat. I needed him inside me, right then, but he didn't seem in a hurry to oblige. Instead he proceeded to torture me with pleasure. He explored every single part of me except that one place that was desperate for his touch.

'Hunter…' I moaned his name, thinking that I might have to kill him if he didn't put me out of my misery soon.

His tongue trailed maddeningly close to that part of me and I tried to shift my hips but his hands clamped tight on my thighs, holding me trapped and still so that I was totally at his mercy.

'Please—please…' It was more of a moan than coherent speech but he must have got the message, because finally I felt his fingers part me, felt his tongue dip inside me, caressing with unerring accuracy and wicked skill until I was almost sobbing with the sheer overload of pleasure. I was so close, *so close,* my hunger for him wild and out of control, but he held me on the edge of it, refusing to give me what I needed.

Through the pounding of blood in my ears I heard the scrape of the stool on the tiled floor as he stood up, a crash as it fell, but neither of us took any notice. I don't think we would have noticed if the roof had fallen in, because the only thing that mattered to us right there and then was what we were doing to each other.

His mouth was on mine and he was kissing me with raw, sensual demand. Finally he let go of my hips, but only so that he could pull a condom out of his pocket.

I tried to help, but that simply slowed things down and I heard him curse softly as he gently pushed my fumbling fingers out of the way and dealt with it himself.

His mouth was still on mine and he sank his hands beneath me, hauled me off the counter so that my legs were wrapped around his waist and sank into me with a deep thrust. I dug my nails hard into the thick muscle of his shoulders. I'd forgotten how big he was and just for a moment I wondered how this was all going to work, but I was so wet, so ready for him, it was as if we'd been designed to fit perfectly together. My body tightened around his and he groaned deep in his throat, an earthy primal sound that told me everything I needed to know about the way he was feeling. And I was feeling the same way. I couldn't breathe. I was drowning in sensation, knowing I'd never, ever felt like this before, not even the first time we were together.

He just stayed without moving and I could feel the thickness of him, the strength and power deep inside me. I rested my forehead against his and our eyes held. That connection was every bit as intimate as the merging of our bodies. I had no idea how he was managing to hold back, because I was ready to explode. I discovered that anticipation could be painful. That needing someone could drive me almost to screaming pitch. And then he withdrew and thrust deep again and after that, control ceased to exist for either of us. He filled me, drove into me, dominated me, until the world outside ceased to exist and the only thing that mattered was what we shared. His mouth was hot and skilled, each forceful thrust of his body sending me closer and closer to ecstasy. Sex between us had always been good but never, ever had it been like this. We climaxed together, the pleasure a relentless, overpowering rush that consumed us both and left us fighting for air.

Holy crap.

My arms were locked around his shoulders, now slick with sweat, and I felt the scrape of stubble as he dragged his mouth from mine and kissed my neck, his breathing rough and uneven.

I closed my eyes, trying to find my sense of balance.

A faint flicker of unease rippled beneath the soporific pleasure that followed the storm.

I'd told myself this was just sex. But there was no 'just' anything when I was with Hunter. Everything was intense and exaggerated and the whole lethal mix of the man and my feelings threatened more than my equilibrium.

I heard him inhale.

'That was…' He stopped midway through the sentence, only I knew in his case it was because he was struggling.

'Yeah.'

'How long since—?'

'None of your business.'

I waited for him to say something but he didn't. I waited for him to put me down, but he didn't do that either. Instead he eased away from me, but only so that he could shift my position slightly and grab the champagne and glasses—with one hand. Don't try this at home. Then he carried me out of the kitchen.

It was a bit caveman.

Still wrapped around him, I pressed my mouth to his face. 'You Tarzan, me Jane.'

'Hi, Jane. Want to get naked with me?'

'I think we already did that bit. Where are we going?'

'I'm going to show you my loincloth.'

We were both laughing but even laughter didn't lessen the sexual high, and then we were in his bedroom and he set me down on the bed, which was a relief because my legs felt so weak I wasn't sure they'd hold me if he'd expected me to stand.

Somehow he managed to put the champagne and the glasses down without spilling anything and turned to face me.

'This time,' he said slowly, 'we're going to do it properly.'

I wondered what he thought we'd just done.

CHAPTER EIGHT

HIS BEDROOM FACED over the river and I could see the London Eye in the distance. I imagined all the tourists in those glass pods training their binoculars on the Houses of Parliament and Buckingham Palace and catching sight of Hunter naked in his apartment. He was more impressive than any London landmark—but he didn't offer two-for-one tickets, so you can forget any ideas about increasing visitor numbers.

I sat on his bed, naked apart from the pink T-shirt, and he was still dressed.

I believed in equality. 'Take your clothes off.'

That made him smile. 'I hoped you might do it for me.'

'That works for me. What did you mean when you said we were going to do it properly?'

He topped up our glasses. 'We're going to take our time. We have five years to catch up on, Ninja.'

Despite all my protests, the name made my insides melt.

It was personal.

It was ours.

Something of the past that locked us together and made this more than a mindless sexual encounter. Nothing could change the fact we had history.

He handed me a glass and I sat up on his bed and took it. I'm not much of a drinker generally, because I'm so serious about training. It didn't take more than a few gulps before I could feel a warmth slowly spreading through my limbs. Or maybe it was being close to him.

Keeping his eyes on me, he dragged off his shirt.

My gaze slid upward to his shoulders, power-packed muscle. He'd always had a good body, but the years and intense training had added definition.

His jeans were undone at the waist and a line of dark hair guided the eye downward.

My mouth was dry and I took a mouthful of champagne and then put the glass down and shifted across the bed so I was eye level with the thick ridge of his erection, which was as big as the rest of him.

Looking up at him, I slid my hands round the bare

skin of his back and then pushed his jeans past his hips and down his legs.

Hunter had been my first and they say you always remember your first, but even if he hadn't been, he wasn't a man any woman was likely to forget.

He was perfect to look at and I devoured him greed-ily with my eyes before leaning forward and taking the whole hot, hard, smooth length of him into my mouth.

His breathing changed and it gave me a feeling of satisfaction to know I affected him as deeply as he af-fected me.

I took my time. Exploring him with the tip of my tongue, taking him deep, teasing him until he groaned and sank his hands into my hair. I felt the hard bite of his fingers against my scalp and then he eased away from me, flattened me to the bed and came down on top of me.

'I want you again.' His voice was thickened, his eyes dark and dangerous as he held my gaze.

'I want you, too.'

He kissed his way along my cheek to my mouth and I felt the rough scrape of his jaw against my skin. My stomach tensed with anticipation. I didn't understand how I could want him again so badly after what we'd just done.

He slid his hands to my hips and flipped me over. I

felt his hand slide down my spine, linger on the curve of my bottom and then slide between my thighs and I closed my eyes because he knew exactly where to touch me, exactly how to drive me wild.

He pulled me up so that I was on my knees, anchored my hips with his hands and slid deep. I closed my eyes. I couldn't see him but my erotic imagination soared into overdrive. I could visualise how we must look, him with those powerful thighs pressed hard up against mine so there was no space between us. Me, my hair tumbling forward over my face, my bottom lifted to him as I knelt before him like some pagan sacrifice. He drew back and then thrust again and I moaned, feeling every inch of him. I was so aroused, so sensitised, the pleasure close to agonising. My neck was damp with sweat, my whole body trembling with every deliberate thrust. I knew I wasn't going to last. He knew it, too, but this time it seemed he wasn't going to make me wait. Or maybe he was the one who didn't want to wait, because he reached forward and slid those skilled, expert fingers over my slick flesh. The first ripple of my orgasm drew a groan from deep in his throat. I felt myself tighten around him and then my loss of control became his and he erupted in a forceful climax, holding me tightly as he buried himself deep.

It was primal, primitive and nothing like anything we'd shared before.

Afterward I didn't think I was capable of moving. I felt wrung out, shattered and a bit stunned but he eased away from me, rolled me over and came down on top of me, his gaze fixed on mine with disturbing intensity.

I stared up at him, trying to look cool about the whole thing, but I felt as if I'd suffered a direct hit from a meteorite. I couldn't move, couldn't think, so when he reached across and pulled another condom out of the drawer by his bed, I gave a whimper of protest.

'Hunter, I can't. I'm too sensitive. You can't possibly be able to— Oh…'

He slid his hand under me and this time he entered me slowly, by degrees, taking his time, proving once again that his self-control was so much better developed than mine, and I discovered I wasn't too sensitive. I discovered that sex with Hunter was an addiction I wasn't likely to recover from anytime soon.

I wrapped my legs around him, slid my hands up his chest and stroked my hands over the hard bulge of his biceps.

The excitement was almost unbearable and I knew he felt it, too, because he kept his eyes on mine the whole time, which made the whole experience more intimate. There was no way either of us could not know who we were with. He was as into me as I was him. Our mouths fused, his tongue stroked mine and he thrust deeper. Dimly, in the back of my mind, I realised I was in trouble. I was supposed to be getting him out of my system. I was supposed to be detached and just interested in sex, but this felt like so much more than that. I tried to grab hold of that thought and work out just how much trouble I was in, but his hand cupped my face as he surged into me again and again, adjusting the angle until the whole of me was flooded with intense white heat. With every skilled stroke, he proved just how well he knew me and I moaned his name, losing all hope of playing it cool or hiding my feelings. He was so strong, so masculine in every way and everything we did was on a different level.

I felt myself tighten around him, heard him swear under his breath as my body gripped his and we both lost control at the same moment. I held on to his broad shoulders, battered by the powerful surge of pleasure, swamped by a wash of sensation that threatened to drown me. He lowered his mouth to mine and we kissed right through it so that there wasn't a single part of us that wasn't involved and engaged.

Total sex, I thought. I'd given all of me. Everything. *Everything except my heart.*

We stayed like that for a long time, his weight crushing me, my arms holding on to him. Then he seemed to realise he was probably too heavy and he rolled onto his back and took me with him so I was curved against him. His arm kept me locked against his side. My head rested on his shoulder, which basically meant I was staring at his chest. Women probably would have bought tickets to see this view.

His arm tightened. 'I missed you.'

It was the last thing I expected him to say and I closed my eyes tightly, trying to push back the emotions that threatened to engulf me.

'Really? Because I hardly noticed you were gone.'

'So Hayley was lying when she said you cried every night for six months?'

I sensed from his tone he was smiling. 'She was exaggerating. She always exaggerates.'

'No, she doesn't. She's a scientist. She bases everything on fact. She said you lost weight.'

'That was intentional. I was training hard.'

There was a brief pause. His grip on me tightened. 'I'm sorry I made you cry, Ninja.'

'I'm not. If it hadn't been for you, I never would have dated men like Brian and think what I would have missed.' I made light of it because the alternative was getting heavy and I didn't want that, but when I tried to sit up he held me tightly.

'I hurt you.'

'I don't really want to talk about this.'

'Why?'

'Because if we talk about it, I have to remember my awful behaviour.'

He rolled onto his side and looked at me, a frown on his face. 'Awful?'

'I was so needy. I smothered you.'

'You were having a difficult time.' He stroked my hair back from my face. 'How are things with your parents now?'

'Okay. We don't see that much of them. I have Hayley and we have a great group of friends. I suppose our friends are our family. I'm sorry for my parents.' It had taken a long time to feel that way, but it was true. 'They were so wrong for each other. They just made each other miserable.'

'And they made you miserable.'

I shrugged. 'Plenty of people are fucked up by their families.'

'That's true.'

I realised I didn't know much about his family. He'd told me once that his mother had left when he was young and that he'd lived with his father. It had all sounded pretty normal to me, but most things were compared to my crazy, dysfunctional family. I realised now that my own altered perspective had stopped me asking more questions. 'Were you?'

His grip tightened. 'I was fine.'

That wasn't enough for me. I wanted to know more. Last time we'd been together I'd been focused on my own issues, but now I'd moved on and I wanted to know about him. 'Was that why you spent so much time at the gym? Because home was grim?' At the time I hadn't even questioned it. I'd been so focused on myself and my own problems I hadn't thought to question why he'd spent so much time at the gym. I'd presumed it was because martial arts were his passion.

He rolled onto his back and sat up. 'Do you want some food?'

I wasn't really listening.

I was remembering what he'd said on that first day, about everyone having something in their lives. At the time I'd been so swamped in my own misery I hadn't picked up on it.

'I want you to talk to me.'

'I need something to eat.' Without looking at me, he pulled on his jeans and strolled out of the room to the kitchen and I sensed he wasn't walking away because he was hungry.

I realised now that when we'd been together, I'd been the one to do all the talking.

I slid out of bed, too, pulled on my shirt and followed him into the kitchen.

'When we were together, you never talked about yourself.'

Without looking at me, he turned the heat up under the pan. 'You had enough worries of your own. And anyway, talking doesn't help.'

'It did for me.'

'Good. It's important to know what works.'

'I want to talk about you for a change.'

He didn't turn. 'Talking doesn't change the facts.'

'But knowing the facts can sometimes help someone understand.'

'What do you want to understand?'

In my head there was a vision of him squatting down in front of the little boy in the gym. Hunter Black, who had trained stars in Hollywood, giving all his attention to a child who was being bullied.

'Tell me about your family.' I pushed my hair away from my face, conscious that wild sex had left it tangled and messy. 'I mean, do they even know you're back? Have you told them?'

'There's no one to tell. My mother lives in Spain now.'

'What about your dad? You once told me your dad was the reason you took up karate.'

'He was. Indirectly.' He picked up the eggs he'd abandoned earlier. 'Omelette all right with you?'

'Fine, thanks. What do you mean, "indirectly"?'

There was a long pause and then a sizzle as the eggs hit the pan. 'He hit my mother. She sent me to karate so I would be able to defend myself if something happened to her. She saved what little money he let her have and spent it on lessons for me.' He paused. 'I went because I wanted to be able to defend her, which was a pretty big ambition for someone of that age.'

'Oh my God.'

It wasn't what I'd expected him to say.

I stared at his broad bare shoulders, not knowing how to respond. Remembering how protective he'd been of me, it was all too easy to imagine he would have been the same with his mother. 'How old were you?'

He tilted the pan. 'Four.'

My heart tightened. 'You were *four* when he hit you?'

'No, I was four when I started karate. I don't remember when he first hit me but I do remember my mother pushing me into a cupboard to protect me and locking the door.'

My heart was pounding. The horror of it engulfed me like a grey, dirty wave. 'She did that?'

'She hid the key so he couldn't get me, but he

knocked her out and they took her to hospital without realising I was in the cupboard.' He reached for two plates and divided the omelette, as if we were talking about our plans for the summer, not something that had formed him.

'How long were you in there?'

'They kept her in the hospital overnight.'

I thought of him, four years old and trapped in the dark. I remembered what he'd said about not liking enclosed spaces and suddenly his choice of apartment made sense. Not just because it was above the business but because it was a collision of light and space. No one could ever feel trapped here. 'What happened? Did your mother leave him?'

'Eventually. Not soon enough. I was eleven. It wasn't easy for her. She'd had a rough life and she saw him as security. He used that to manipulate her. He made her feel as if she wouldn't be able to survive without him. In the end being without him was the only way she could survive.' He handed me a plate and I took it without even looking at the food.

'And she left you with him?'

'She made the right choice. It was about survival.'

'Were you angry with her for leaving you?'

'No. I was relieved. The responsibility was crushing. It had got to the point where I was afraid to leave her alone in the house with him. It meant I only had myself to worry about.'

I tried to imagine how that must have felt, being a young boy and feeling responsible for the safety of your mother.

I looked at him. The food on my plate remained untouched.

I realised how little I'd known about him. How little I'd asked.

'Where is your dad now?'

'He died a few years ago. Cirrhosis, which was a surprise to no one given that his longest relationship was with the contents of a whisky bottle.'

'And your mum?'

'She's safe. And happy. She met someone.' His voice softened and I felt something squeeze inside me.

I wondered how he'd handled it so well.

He added a chunk of fresh bread to his plate but I shook my head when he offered me the same.

'No, thanks.'

'You need carbs.'

'I'm not hungry.' What he'd told me had taken away my appetite. 'You never told me any of this.'

'It was history by the time I met you.'

But it explained why he'd always seemed so strong and self-reliant. He'd had to be.

We took the plates back to bed and finished the food and the champagne.

I looked at my phone and realised it was 2 a.m. 'It's late. I should go.'

'Stay the night.' His tone was rough and I looked at him, sorely tempted.

Hayley wasn't home. She'd texted me earlier to say she was staying at Nico's for the weekend. Also that she was borrowing my favourite shoes because she was accompanying him to some smart lawyer do.

There was no reason to go and plenty of reasons to stay. Like the way Hunter was looking at me and the slow, seductive brush of his fingers over my arm. My skin was super sensitive, my insides melting.

It wasn't as if we'd exactly denied ourselves. There was no reason to feel this desperate, but still I was desperate.

I'd always thought my willpower was pretty good. I could resist chocolate and biscuits, but it turned out I couldn't resist Hunter.

He was my weakness.

'I don't have anything with me.'

'I have everything you're likely to need.'

That was what worried me.

I pushed that thought aside and slid out of bed. Then I picked up the plates and took them to the kitchen, telling myself that it was fine to stay. That I could cope with it. That my emotions were under control.

If you want to justify something, it's pretty much always possible if you work hard at it. But the only real justification as far as I was concerned was that I wanted to.

I was having the best time of my life.

Why not?

CHAPTER NINE

'COFFEE?'

I woke to find sun streaming through the windows and Hunter standing next to me, a towel knotted around his hips, his hair wet from the shower.

Groaning, I sat up and pushed my hair away from my face. 'You were up early.'

'It's ten o'clock.' He handed me the coffee. 'Not that early.'

'Ten? You're kidding.' I reached for my phone, saw that he was telling the truth and felt heat rise in my cheeks. 'I was tired.'

'I think I might know the reason for that.' His tone was a soft masculine purr that made me want to ditch the coffee and drag him back into bed.

My muscles ached in places they hadn't ached for

ages. Thanks to him, I was aware of every part of my body.

I sipped my coffee and then put it down on the table next to the bed, feeling suddenly awkward. After last time, I was determined not to do anything that could be defined as clinging. 'I should get going. I expect you have plans.'

'My plans include you.'

I probably should have played it very cool and made some excuse about needing to be at home, but as I opened my mouth to speak, I turned my head and the words jammed in my throat. The towel had slipped slightly, revealing even more of the hard, honed abs and the powerful muscles of his chest and arms.

I told myself that any woman who would be able to walk away from that needed therapy.

'What did you have in mind?'

He gave a slow smile and I smiled, too, because it was obvious how we were going to spend the weekend.

I reached out and tugged at the towel, but he was already coming down on top of me, pulling the covers back, exposing me.

I slept naked, so there wasn't much chance of hiding, not that I wanted to.

Sunshine fell across the bed, spotlighting my body and his. He lowered his head, plundering my lips and then moving lower. He took his time, driving me mad, tormenting me with every skilled flick of his tongue. He didn't just know how to kiss my mouth; he knew how to kiss all of me and he employed those skills with devastating effect on my breasts and then lower to the damp, swollen heart of me. The pleasure spread through me in hot waves and he teased and tormented me until I was writhing on the bed and then he locked his hands on my hips and forced me to lie still while he took his time and explored me with merciless skill. My body was his playground and by the time he pulled me under him I was almost sobbing with desperation.

He paused for a moment, looking down at me, and then he sank into me, driving deep into the heart of me with unleashed hunger. If he'd held back last time, he certainly didn't this time. My hands moved to his shoulders and I felt the ripple of muscle under my fingers, felt the hard strength of him as he pulled back and then drove deep. My hands slid lower and closed over the hard bulge of his biceps. His eyes held mine and he lowered his forehead to mine and then kissed me, biting at my lips, nibbling and driving me crazy while all the time his body possessed mine.

I was consumed by sensation and so was he. Excitement spiralled around us, drawing us closer, spinning a web that locked us together.

He dominated me, drove into me with a relentless perfect rhythm until we both hit the same peak at the same time and exploded together in an overload of pleasure.

The wildness of it shocked me and I think it shocked him a bit, too, because he rolled onto his back and folded me into his arms and held me there until both of us could breathe properly again.

'Why didn't you stay in Hollywood?' I lay there filled with questions, wanting to uncover every secret, every hidden corner of him that I didn't already know.

'I enjoy coaching. Hollywood was a means to an end. I earned enough to be able to buy this place.'

'And a cool car.'

'That, too.'

I asked him again about Thailand. He asked me about everything I'd been doing. We had a huge gap in our history and we filled it in together, learning, discovering. We were filling in the blanks. Joining the dots.

We lay in bed, made love and talked. We talked about things we'd never talked about when we were together the first time. I didn't even check my phone, because I was absorbed and time wasn't relevant.

We spent the whole weekend in bed.

He rang for takeout food and walked downstairs

to the door to collect it, but apart from that we didn't leave his apartment.

The hunger in him matched mine.

I might have missed the fact it was Sunday night had a text not come through from Hayley. 'I forgot to buy batteries but as I haven't heard from you, I guess you don't need them. :)'

I was about to switch my phone off when another text came. 'Be careful.'

I knew she wasn't talking about the sex. She was talking about my heart.

And I realised I'd put myself at risk again. 'Just sex' didn't mean spending an entire weekend with a guy, talking about every subject under the sun. It wasn't getting to know him and wanting to know all the small things. But that was how I felt with Hunter. I wanted to know every corner of him. I wasn't interested in superficial; I wanted depth.

I just couldn't help myself around him. I couldn't stop myself falling.

Hunter was watching me, sensing the change. 'Are you all right, Ninja?'

The endearment cracked me wide open and I realised in a rush of panic that I'd been kidding myself. This wasn't just sex. With Hunter it never had been and it probably never could be.

I'd thought that if our relationship was just about sex, I couldn't be hurt but when my heart was involved? That was different. That made me vulnerable.

I wouldn't allow it to happen to me again.

I had to protect myself.

'I have to go.' I shot out of bed without looking at him and rummaged for my clothes. 'Hayley is at home.'

'She's not a kid.' His voice was soft. 'She doesn't need a babysitter.'

And I realised then that there was no point in being anything but honest, so I turned, clutching my shirt against me.

'I can't do this, Hunter. I thought I could, but I can't.'

He was very still. 'Which bit can't you do?'

Love, I thought silently. *I can't do love.* Not when it was one-sided. Not when all the feelings were mine.

'This. Us. It's going to make our working relationship awkward. People are already noticing and talking about us.'

'Let them talk.'

'It isn't a good idea to sleep with the boss.'

'I'm the boss and it seems like a good idea to me.'

Whatever I said, he countered, pressing closer and closer to the truth, but I'd learned my lesson. This time around, my feelings were my problem, not his.

I wasn't going to dump them all over him again, as I had the first time.

'Well, I'm the employee and it's awkward for me. This has been fun, but it was a one-time thing. Just the weekend. From tomorrow we're back to being how we were.'

'And how were we?'

'Colleagues. I don't want to be intimate.' But I realised that we'd never been anything but intimate, and with that admission came the unpalatable realisation that I was probably going to have to leave my job because I was never, ever going to feel normal around this man. I wasn't capable of feeling indifferent. 'Just colleagues.'

He gave me a long steady look. 'Are you sure that's what you want?'

'I'm sure.' I made for the door before he could see through the lies. Last time I'd smothered him in my feelings. This time I was going to spare him that. 'I'll see you at work tomorrow.'

I limped through the next few weeks, pretending I was fine. Every minute was torture. I gritted my teeth and counted down the hours until the weekend, when I didn't have to see him.

Three weeks after I'd done the 'let's be colleagues' speech, I was lying in bed with the duvet over my head pretending to be asleep when I heard my sister open the door.

Hayley wasn't fooled. We'd shared a room growing up, so she always knew when I was asleep and when I was faking.

I felt the bed dip as she sat down.

'I have coffee, an untouched packet of chocolate biscuits or a glass of wine. You pick.'

I didn't answer. I hoped she'd go away, but of course, this was my sister, so there was no hope of that. Instead the duvet was tugged from my fingers and she wriggled into the bed and snuggled under the covers with me.

'Do you want to talk about it?'

I would have thought the duvet over my head would have answered that question, but Hayley wasn't easy to deflect. 'I'm fine.'

'Right. Because not eating, sleeping or laughing is totally you, as is spending an entire Saturday in bed.'

I wanted to say something flippant but my throat was clogged with misery. I hadn't allowed myself to cry, but suddenly I was crying and my sister was holding me and she was muttering 'Shh' and 'I'm going to kill the bastard' as she stroked my hair.

'Not his fault. My fault for loving the wrong man.' I choked out the words but it didn't stop her listing all the dire methods of torture she had in mind for Hunter Black.

'You're crazy about him. You always have been.'

And suddenly I was telling her everything. How it had been at work, about that weekend, all of it. 'When I'm with him, I can be myself. I never feel as if I'm being judged. He likes me the way I am. He doesn't want me to join a book group or learn to bake cupcakes. He doesn't care that I have a flat chest or that I like practising my kicks while we're talking.' I scrubbed my face with my hand and sat upright. My head throbbed from crying. 'And he makes me laugh.'

My sister looked at my swollen face and raised her eyebrows. 'You're not laughing now.'

'That's not his fault.'

'Have you told him how you feel?'

'After last time?' I grabbed a tissue and blew my nose. 'No way.'

'Maybe he feels the same way you do.'

'No. For him it was just about fun and sex. That's how I wanted it to be, too!' I shredded the tissue. 'I'm going to have to leave my job.'

'You love working there!'

'Not anymore. It's too hard. Too awkward and I don't want to embarrass him a second time. I'm going to look for something else. And I know that makes me pathetic, but—'

'It doesn't make you pathetic.' Her phone beeped to indicate a text but she ignored it. 'You need to leave this bed and come out with us tonight.'

I managed a smile. 'Just because I can't get my own sex life sorted out, doesn't mean I want to ruin yours. Go. Nico is texting you.' I gave her a push. 'Go and have fun. You can borrow my shoes if you like. I don't need them.'

I couldn't imagine ever wanting to go out again.

She slid out of the bed and paused in the doorway. 'I still think you should tell Hunter how you feel.'

'This time around, it's my problem. I'll handle it.'

But handling it drained me.

Every time I saw him approaching, I dived for cover and I stayed later and later to avoid leaving at the same time as him, but he left late, too, because he was the boss.

I stopped going to staff nights out, then decided not going made it look as if I was avoiding him, so I went and pretended to have fun on the dance floor. I concentrated so hard on 'having fun' I almost sprained my ankle.

Proving I was fine was exhausting. My smile muscles were getting a more rigorous workout than my abs or my thighs.

And then finally I heard I had an interview at a fitness club closer to home.

I should have been thrilled. Provided I didn't mess up the interview, this nightmare would be over. And then I realised taking this job would mean I wouldn't see Hunter again. He really would be out of my life.

And that was the biggest nightmare of all.

'What are you doing for your birthday, Rosie?' Caroline stuffed her bag into the locker and pulled out her water bottle.

'I'm having a quiet night.' I was going to hide under the duvet and hope that when I woke up a year older, I'd be cured of the way I was feeling.

But my sister was having none of it.

'You are not spending another Saturday night in bed watching TV. That's not happening. I've planned you a surprise party.'

'I really don't—'

'Shut up and get dressed in something warm. Wear that gorgeous coat you bought last winter. The short, sexy black one that makes you look like a Russian princess.' She was checking her phone. 'We need to go. Cab's outside.'

For my sister's sake I washed my hair and dragged

on my clothes. The black coat was a perfect contrast to my white face. I felt like crap and I looked like crap. I knew I needed to snap out of it. I was no fun to be with. And it was no one's fault but my own. I'd played with fire. I'd been burned. Again.

Hayley bundled me into the cab and handed the driver our destination on a piece of paper so I couldn't see.

'Don't you think you're taking this a bit far? I've lived in London all my life. I'll know where we're going.'

'No, you won't.' She pulled a scarf out of her bag and tied it around my eyes while I protested.

'Oh for...' I thought it was overkill. 'You'll smudge my makeup.'

'I want it to be a surprise.'

'The surprise is going to be me looking as if I'm dressed for Halloween. Who is coming, anyway?'

'Our friends.' It was a suspiciously vague answer and I was starting to feel exhausted when she tugged off the scarf.

'We're here.'

And in spite of everything, I smiled, because we were right next to the London Eye, my favourite place.

'You booked a night flight? That's perfect.' I could see our friends gathered waiting and I felt a warmth spread through me. It was the closest I'd come to feeling happy since I'd broken it off with Hunter.

I still had my sister. I still had friends. I'd got over him before. I'd get over him again.

I could learn to live without breath-stealing excitement. I could afford extra batteries.

We tumbled out of the cab and our friends swarmed around us. I was handed lots of interesting parcels and bags that my sister took away and tucked in a larger bag she'd brought with her.

'You can have them later.'

'What's wrong with now? I can open them during the flight.'

'You should be looking at the view and concentrating on the stuff that matters. Like my gift to you. It's waiting in the capsule.' She leaned forward and hugged me. 'Happy birthday, Rosie. I hope it's a special one.'

'Why have you left my gift in the capsule? Someone might steal it. What is it?'

She pulled away from me and gave me a long look, a smile and then a little push. 'Go on, birthday girl. Find out.'

Still looking at my sister, wondering what she'd bought me, I climbed the steps. I was expecting her to follow but she just stood there in the middle of our friends, watching with a smile on her face. I knew something was going on but I had no idea what.

Only when I stepped into the capsule did I turn my head.

Hunter stood there, with his back to the view, watching me.

'Happy birthday, Ninja.'

CHAPTER TEN

I STARED AT him, felt a flicker of panic and then turned quickly to find my sister and the others but the attendant was sealing our capsule and the rest of my group were on the other side of the barrier, watching avidly.

My eyes met Hayley's accusingly and she blew me a kiss.

I'd assumed my present was a trip on the London Eye, but I realised now her gift was Hunter. We were about to spend thirty minutes suspended over the city in our own private glass bubble. Just the two of us. Thirty minutes during which I had to hide how I felt about him. It was going to be the longest thirty minutes of my life.

It was probably going to be the longest thirty minutes of his life, too.

I felt awkward.

He'd obviously been manipulated into it by my sister, but he probably thought I was behind it because it was just the sort of stunt I would have pulled at eighteen if I'd had the funds. 'I'm sorry. I knew nothing about this. You should have said no.'

'Do you wish I had?'

I gave a casual shrug. 'I love having friends around me on my birthday, but I'm sure there are a million other places you'd rather be. This was Hayley's idea.' I wanted to smile, but honestly, my face was exhausted. I had no idea why fake smiling was so much more tiring than real smiling but it was. I just couldn't do it anymore.

'No, it wasn't. It was my idea.'

The capsule was slowly rising upward but I wasn't looking at the view; I was looking at him. 'Yours?'

'I know how much you love the London Eye. I thought it was time we talked.'

'I see you every day at work.' I was going to kill Hayley for agreeing, but I wasn't going to be able to kill her until the capsule had finished its circle, which meant that for the next half an hour I was locked in an enclosed space with Hunter.

'You've been avoiding me.'

'I've been busy.'

'But now you're not busy, so you can listen to what I have to say.'

'Sure.' I shrugged and strolled to the glass, pretending to look at the view. I kept my back to him. Easier to control my body language that way.

It bothered me that just occupying the same space as him could have this effect on me.

The capsule rose slowly and I could see London spread out beneath our feet. Lights flickered across the dark surface of the river. It would have been captivating if I hadn't been a captive. I saw his reflection in the glass and knew he was standing right behind me.

'I want to talk about why I left.'

'I already know. I was clingy.'

'That isn't why.' He curved his hands over my shoulders and I wished there were an emergency exit or something, because the last thing I wanted or needed was to think about that time in my life. I'd die of embarrassment and I was pretty sure it wasn't going to be good for tourism having a corpse in this capsule.

'We don't need to talk about this. I don't blame you. I understand.'

'No, you don't understand.' His tone was raw and his hands tightened on my shoulders. 'I didn't leave because I didn't care. You didn't drive me away. I left because I knew it was the right thing to do. But leaving was the hardest thing I've ever done.'

I stood still. 'It was hard?'

'I was crazy about you.'

My stomach curled. I felt a wild flutter of excitement that I killed instantly. 'That makes no sense.'

'When we met, you were vulnerable. Lonely and, yes, pretty messed up. I wasn't sure of your feelings.' He breathed deeply. 'You were emotionally raw. Would you have wanted to be with me if that hadn't been the case?'

I wondered how he could possibly have come to that conclusion. 'I was crazy about you, too. We spent every minute together.'

'Exactly.' He paused, his mouth tight. 'And I didn't want that responsibility. It didn't feel right to me. It was too close to what my mother did. And yes, I was scared. I was afraid of letting you down, of failing you.'

'So you went to Thailand?'

'There were plenty of other places I could have trained, Rosie.' He turned me gently so I was forced to look at him. 'Why do you think I picked Thailand?'

'Because you wanted to get as far away from me as possible.'

He gave a humourless laugh. 'You're so wrong about that.'

'You always wanted to train in Thailand.'

'Train, yes. Not move there.' His tone was raw. 'I did it because I loved you and I wasn't good for you. I left because I knew if I didn't, we'd start it up again.'

My knees were shaking. 'You loved me?'

'You know I did.'

'No, I didn't know! You never said.'

'Maybe not those exact words, but I thought it was obvious. Do you remember your eighteenth birthday?'

'Vaguely.' I saw him smile and I couldn't help it—I smiled, too. *Crap.* I was hopeless at playing it cool. 'Oh, all right, yes, I remember it. Mostly because you drove too fast.' And because he'd made it special. Every kiss, every stroke, every gentle touch, had made sure my first time would be the best. The way he'd held my head as he'd kissed me, taken his slow, thorough time to take our relationship to the next level. 'We had sex. It was no big deal.' It had been the biggest deal of my life.

'Everything changed. Our relationship was so serious, so intense. You were so afraid to go and live your life. Instead you clung to the safe option, the familiar.'

'Now we're getting to the embarrassing bit,' I muttered, but he simply smiled and scooped my face into his hands. What I saw in his eyes made me dizzy. 'I don't blame you for going to Thailand, although it was a long way to go to avoid me.'

'I wasn't avoiding you. I didn't trust myself. I knew if you were there, under my nose, I'd want you back. I knew what I wanted.' His voice was raw. 'It was you I wasn't sure of. I wasn't sure you knew what you wanted and then you started giving things up for me and that made my decision.'

'What about my decision?' Anger flickered. 'You could have said all this and I could have told you what I thought. And anyway, you're talking rubbish. I didn't give anything up.'

'You gave up your college place so that you could stay with me.'

I felt my cheeks heat. 'I wasn't that bothered about college.'

'And now you have a degree in physiology and sports science. Would you have had that if I'd stayed?'

I swallowed. 'Probably not. After you left, I gave up on men and surrounded myself with friends. I lived my life, dated guys like Brian. Guys who were nothing like you.'

There was a brief pause. 'And how did that work out?'

I could have lied, but I didn't see the point. 'Pretty crap. Most men don't like me practising my turning kicks on a date.'

'I'm sorry about the way I did it. I'm sorry I hurt you.'

He'd torn me off him like a piece of sticky tape—
quickly. I saw now it had been the right thing to do.

'That's the past.' I used the words he'd used to me
all those years before and I could see in his eyes he remembered.

'Good. Because I want us to start again. And I want
to know how you feel about me.'

I thought about my dreams, the images that rolled
around my head tormenting me when I was supposed
to be sleeping. 'My feelings are my problem.' My voice
was soft, although goodness knows why, because we
were suspended above the river Thames and no one
could hear us. 'I'll deal with them.'

'Tell me.'

I gripped the rail and stared down at London sparkling beneath us. It felt surreal. It felt as if we were
on a magic carpet, flying over the city. 'We've always
had something special....' I kept my eyes forward, not
looking at him, because I was trying to be measured
and not gush all over him. 'Sex is part of that, yes, but
for me there's more. I can't just switch off everything
else and you don't want that. You don't want someone
loving you and I understand that after what you saw
with your mother.'

'What my mother shared with my father wasn't love.
It was an unbalanced, inequitable relationship with all

the control on my father's side.' His voice hardened. 'He sapped her of confidence until she believed she couldn't exist without him. That's not how we are.'

'We?'

He slid his hand behind my neck and I felt his fingers, strong and warm against the nape. 'I want all of it, Ninja.' His voice was low and sexy. 'I want the good and the bad, the exciting and the mundane. I want to prop you up when you feel low, hold you when you're sad and fight your battles.'

He was throwing my own words back at me and I stood for a moment, mesmerised by the look in his eyes.

'I learned how to do those things for myself.' I was trembling. 'I fight my own battles. I comfort myself when I'm low. I have a secret stash of chocolate for that purpose.'

The corners of his mouth flickered. 'Being able to do those things for yourself doesn't stop someone else doing them alongside you. I don't just want sex, Rosie. I love you.'

My knees were shaking. He'd called me Rosie, not Ninja. He'd said— 'You love me? But when—how—when—?' Oh, God, now I was doing it. Not finishing my sentences.

'"When" is easy to answer. I fell in love with you when you climbed on the back of my motorbike. I tried to get you out of my system. Maybe I did for a while, but when I saw you in the restaurant that night, I knew my feelings were as strong as ever. As for the why—' he gave a half smile '—how long have you got?'

My heart was pumping. 'How long do you need?'

He glanced out of the capsule and judged the time left before we arrived back at the beginning. 'I'll give you the highlights. I love your sense of humour. I love the way you laugh so hard you can't stop yourself. I love the fact that you can knock me over with a kick if you get your balance right—'

'There's nothing wrong with my balance!'

He slid his arms around me and hauled me hard against him. 'I love how much you love your sister and your friends. I love—'

'Stop!' Feeling as if I were flying, I covered his lips with my fingers and then lifted myself on tiptoe and wrapped my arms round his neck. 'Stop talking and kiss me. I really want you to kiss me because it's magical up here and I want to have this moment to remember always.'

He lowered his head to mine and he kissed me while the world outside sparkled, the lights of London a carpet beneath our feet and the stars above like jewels in a sky of velvet-black. I'd never been this happy, ever. I knew that there were no guarantees. No one knows the future. But right now this was what I wanted. And I wanted it for all the right reasons.

I didn't want Hunter for security; I wanted him for himself. 'I love you, too.' I whispered the words against his mouth and felt him smile against my lips.

When I eventually pulled away, something made me glance down toward the capsule beneath us and I saw my sister and the rest of our friends gazing up at us, grinning like idiots. I could see they were holding a birthday cake and gesturing.

'They're going to eat my cake. I will kill them.' I'd never loved my sister more than I did at that moment.

I was so happy I did a turning kick in the middle of the capsule and almost smacked Hunter in the head.

Amused, he pulled me back into his arms. 'Happy birthday, Ninja.'

'Thank you.' I slid my arms round him, my present. *My gift*. 'This was the best birthday.'

'It isn't over yet. This is just the beginning.'

As he brought his mouth down on mine, I closed my eyes, thinking that if this was the beginning, then the future was looking even better than my birthday cake.

★ ★ ★ ★ ★

Discover more romance at

www.millsandboon.co.uk

- ♥ WIN great prizes in our exclusive competitions
- ♥ BUY new titles before they hit the shops
- ♥ BROWSE new books and REVIEW your favourites
- ♥ SAVE on new books with the Mills & Boon® Bookclub™
- ♥ DISCOVER new authors

PLUS, to chat about your favourite reads, get the latest news and find special offers:

- ▪ Find us on facebook.com/millsandboon
- ▸ Follow us on twitter.com/millsandboonuk
- ♥ Sign up to our newsletter at millsandboon.co.uk

THE
CHATSFIELD®

Enter the intriguing online world of
The Chatsfield and discover secret
stories behind closed doors...

www.thechatsfield.com

Check in online now for your exclusive
welcome pack!